THE CASE OF THE

LITTLE
GREEN
MEN

THE CASE OF THE
LITTLE
GREEN
MEN

by

Mack Reynolds

Surinam Turtle Press

ISBN 13: 978-1-60543-155-0

ISBN 10: 1-60543-155-9

Cover Art: Steve Leialoha
Cover Design: Gavin L. O'Keefe
Preparation: Richard A. Lupoff and Fender Tucker

Surinam Turtle Press #24

THE CASE OF THE LITTLE GREEN MEN

I was thirteen when I found out my dad had written a "real book." To me that was one with a hard cover. I was very familiar with his stories in science fiction magazines and travel articles, but *The Case of the Little Green Men* was a REAL BOOK!

Dad went on to write a good many books, novelettes, and stories, but this has always been one of my favorites. Combining a good mystery with some top-notch science fiction. It does make sense to me as dad started out writing mysteries for the pulp market right after World War II. He never made much of a success at it and it wasn't until his good friend Fredric Brown, a very well respected science fiction writer in the early 1950's, suggested that as he loved reading science fiction, he should try writing it, that his efforts as an author bore fruit.

His vision of the future included such things as pocket computers, a computer network (long before Al Gore invented it) guaranteed minimum income (welfare), and a mobile population long before RV's came into being. He foresaw a "Common Europe," and instant photography pictures (Digital). His forte was politics, economics, and history. His critics admit that he was "innovative," "clever," and "satirical." More praise than is generally heaped upon his contemporaries of the '50s and '60s.

In 1955 I received another thrill when Dad was published in the November 1955 issue of *Playboy* magazine. His story "Burnt Toast" has been reprinted several times and is still one of my favorites.

In 1968 Dad was commissioned to write the first "Star Trek" novel. Although the television series had been a great hit for several years, no attempt had been made to see if there was a reading audience. Dad wrote *Mission to Horatius* at about a 13-year-old's intellectual level. Unfortunately it was discovered the average age of a "Trekkie" was 20 to 35. I've often wondered what would have happened if he had hit on the right age group.

If you find you have enjoyed this book, may I suggest my personal all-time favorite short story "Compounded Interests." Or his North African Trilogy of *Black Man's Burden, Border, Breed nor Birth*, and *The Best Ye Breed*, another first in science fiction as all of his heroes are African-Americans seeking to unite the North African countries into a single entity.

—Emil Reynolds
April 2009

THE CASE OF THE
LITTLE
GREEN
MEN

PREFACE

The detective isn't tough and he isn't even smart and he doesn't prove the case against the killer. And boy doesn't get girl, either. Otherwise, this story is just about like a good many others you've read.

At least it starts the same way. . . . We can't help it if it dissolves into men from Mars, people who believe in spaceships and flying saucers, murders without motive, and heat rays fired by little green men (or were they?).

CHAPTER ONE

HERE WERE THREE of them and they didn't look like bill collectors, so I took my feet off the desk and repeated, "Come in, come right in," more hospitably this time.

In the way of snap impressions, the group was composed of: one, a stuffed shirt who looked like a cartoon of a successful businessman, whose belly was beginning to declare he was middle-aged, whose jowls were too heavy; two, a thin, nervous kid who couldn't have been more than nineteen, whose clothes hung on him as though he were studying to be a burlesque comedian, whose glasses needed changing or he wouldn't have been blinking so much; three, a tall, lanky customer, whom a Hollywood synopsis would have called a *Jimmy Stewart type,* although his grin was a bit more vacuous than Jimmy's.

"Mr. Knight?" the older one asked. His voice bore out my impression—pompous. Except when he spoke, he held his plump lips tightly together, giving him a peevish look about the mouth.

"That's right," I admitted, getting up to go through the formalities. One and two shook hands seriously; three grinned amiably in the process.

Number one said, "My name is Maddigan, James L. Maddigan." He indicated numbers two and three. "This is Mr. Arthur Roget, and this, Mr. Harold Shulman." Shulman was the scrawny one with the glasses and baggy suit.

We went through the rest of the formalities, everyone winding up in chairs, completely exhausting the seating facilities of *Lee and Knight, Private Investigations.* Shulman, weighing the least, was occupying the rickety chair. When all were seated, I cleared my throat professionally and said, "All right, gentlemen, what can I do for you?"

Maddigan was evidently the spokesman. The other two turned their eyes to him and he said, "Are you available, Mr. Knight? That is, available personally for employment?"

"Just by chance," I told him, "I'm between cases, Mr. Maddigan. Not a thing on the fire." Brother, that was no exaggeration.

"Good," Shulman said shrilly. It was the first time he had opened his trap since they had entered.

Maddigan patted his plump right knee to indicate satisfaction. "Yes, very good. And what are your rates, Mr. Knight?"

Until now, I hadn't been sure whether they were clients or not. Believe me, I wasn't expecting business, not after that fiasco of which the newspapers had made such a field day.

I was off-hand. "That's according to the service, Mr. Maddigan. Ordinarily my rates are, uh, twenty-five dollars a day, plus expenses, transportation and so forth. However, there are some assignments—" I left it there.

They passed glances back and forth between themselves.

"That seems satisfactory," Maddigan nodded. He hesitated for a moment, as though wondering how to open the subject. That was out of character; he didn't look as though he ever doubted his ability to reel off instructions to an employee right off the cuff.

He pursed his plump lips and said finally, "We're a committee from the Scylla Club."

That didn't mean anything to me, so I didn't say anything.

He chose his words carefully. "This will undoubtedly sound fantastic to you, Mr. Knight, but I shall come immediately to the point. Some of the members of our organization are of the opinion that there are aliens in the United States."

That called for a worried frown. I'd been practically spending my money; now he come up with a silly remark like that. "Rather obvious, isn't it?" I asked carefully.

"From space," Roget blurted. His easygoing smile was gone and he was leaning forward earnestly, his elbows on his knees, his hands clasped between his legs.

"Hum?" I said.

Maddigan impatiently flicked one of his stubby-fingered hands from side to side. "Let me tell this, Art." He hadn't taken his eyes from me. "We are, some of us at least, Mr. Knight, of the opinion that alien life forms are possibly present in the United States."

I still didn't get it. "You mean like in Buck Rogers, the flying saucers, that sort of thing?"

Young Shulman began shrilly, "That's not exactly the way to put it."

Maddigan silenced him too. "Perhaps we had best start at the beginning, Mr. Knight. Have you read *Life on Other Worlds?*"

I shook my head. "Sounds like something by Edgar Rice Burroughs."

"To the contrary, it was written by H. Spencer Jones, the Astronomer Royal of England." He took a digest-size book from a side pocket. "This is a reprint from his work."

I leaned back, waiting for the worst. He was thumbing through the pocket book looking for some particular passage.

"Ah, yes, this for instance." He began reading. *"With the universe constructed on so vast a scale, it would seem inherently improbable that our small earth can be the only home of life."* He skipped over some more pages. "And here: '. . . *It seems reasonable to suppose that whenever in the universe the proper conditions arise, life must inevitably come into existence. This is the view that is generally accepted by biologists.'* "

He began looking for more passages.

"All right," I told him hurriedly. "I get it. This guy thinks that life is possible on other planets. Who'd you say he was again?"

"The Astronomer Royal of England. And don't misunderstand: not just other planets in the sense of other planets in the solar system. It is quite possible that life, except for some rather simple vegetation on Mars, doesn't exist besides on earth, in *our* solar system. But that doesn't mean that other stars do not have planets that support life."

"Possibly intelligent life," Shulman shrilled excitedly. That voice of his went with his clothes—all he needed was a good straight man and he was a natural for a job at the Old Howard in Boston.

"Yes, definitely," Maddigan said, taking over again. "Do you follow thus far, Mr. Knight? That is, do you realize the possibility that life, even intelligent life, might exist elsewhere in the universe?"

I let my right shoulder lift and drop again, and stirred uncomfortably in my chair. This was the damnedest set of potential clients I'd ever run into. "I suppose anything's possible," I admitted, "and this astronomer guy should know more about it than I do."

"Very well. Now then, if we presuppose intelligent life in the universe besides ours, we must admit one of the following: first, that it is less intelligent, or at least less scientifically advanced than we are; second, that it is just as intelligent and as advanced as we; third, that it is more intelligent and advanced than we."

I essayed a wry grin. "That about covers everything, I imagine. But what's this about there being aliens on earth?"

He held up a commanding hand. "We'll get to that. Now, Mr. Knight, do you realize that the earth is on the verge of space travel?"

"How was that?" He kept throwing these punches so fast I had trouble keeping my feet.

"The earth, and the United States in particular, is on the verge of interplanetary travel. If you kept up with the news of the day, you would know that experiments with rockets of the German V-2 type and even more advanced American models have put us on the threshold of travel, first to the moon, then to our sister planets, Mars and Venus."

I said weakly, "I didn't know it was as near as all that. Of course—"

Roget had been leaning forward earnestly, watching my face for every reaction. "Nearer than most think," he injected. "Willy Ley, one of the top rocket authorities, says that with even our present knowledge we have the know-how to get a rocket to the moon. Why, for all we know, the government might have already done it. If they have, it'd probably be on the top secret list, classified. I think—"

"We're getting away from the point," Maddigan interrupted. Every time one of the younger men got in a word he seemed irritated. "The point is that we ourselves have nearly accomplished space travel. If there are more advanced life forms in the universe, it is very possible that they have achieved it."

I got one of my briers out of the top desk drawer and filled it slowly from the pound tin that sits right next to the telephone. I tamped the tobacco down carefully with my right forefinger, then reached into a coat pocket for my king-size box of kitchen matches—the only lighter I've ever been able to make work—and lit up carefully. It still didn't make sense to me, but at least I was beginning to get their drift.

"Like the flying saucers?" I asked.

Maddigan twisted his beefy shoulders. "Possibly the flying saucers; there are as many different opinions on that phenomenon as there have been saucers sighted. Possibly they aren't extra-terrestrial at all, but even if they're not, it doesn't mean that we haven't had, or do not have now, visitors among us."

"Why?" I asked. "Why should these little green men want to come to earth?"

Maddigan waggled a finger at me. "I am disappointed in you, Mr. Knight," he said peevishly. "This is a subject in which you are little versed. You have admitted almost complete ignorance, but still you are contemptuous. You say jokingly, 'little green men,' and your tone of voice implies that the very thought of alien life is ridiculous. Yet you have no evidence to support your prejudice."

He had me there. I twisted my mouth sourly. "All right, I'll take that. I have no evidence to prove that there aren't alien life forms, as you called them, here on earth. I should keep an open mind until I get evidence one way or the other. By the way, if they aren't green, what color are they? What do they look like?"

Shulman said disgustedly, "How would we know? Possibly they're either humanoid, or have disguised themselves to look like humans." He looked as though he were willing to elaborate on the subject, but Maddigan motioned him to silence and took hold of the conversation again.

"You asked why they should want to come to earth. There might be a multitude of reasons, Mr. Knight, but here is just one, a good one. Let us suppose that you were a member of an advanced race with a civilization far beyond ours. Suppose that for some time you had been observing the progress of mankind from afar, noting his nature, his institutions, his way of conducting himself. Suppose that you observed his discovery of nuclear fission and the manner in which he was utilizing it; and suppose further that you noted that he was about to achieve space travel. What would you do, Mr. Knight?"

I sucked deeply on the pipe, let the smoke dribble from my nostrils and stared up at my dirty ceiling. "I don't know," I told him. "It's according to what kind of people this other intelligent life was. You probably expect me to say that if I was such an alien, I'd destroy the human race before it could get in a position to destroy me."

"As I have said, that is one possibility." He patted his right knee to indicate he'd made his point.

There's nothing like stringing along. I leaned far back in my chair and summarized it: "Thus far, we've assumed that there is conceivably intelligent life in the universe besides man. Then we've assumed that being possibly more advanced in science than we, they have achieved space travel sooner, and consequently, would be able to journey here if they wished. Now what?"

Maddigan beamed at me. "We now get to the point, Mr. Knight. We want to employ you to investigate the presence of such alien life forms."

I had to catch my pipe as it fell from my open mouth. "You want me to *what?*" I hurriedly brushed some live ashes from my pants, staring at him as I did.

"We want you to investigate the possibility of there being alien life forms here on earth." His tone suggested that nothing could be more reasonable.

"You mean you want me to go around looking for men from Mars, for characters out of Orson Welles?"

Maddigan's heavy brows met impatiently. "You said you were available for employment. Why should one assignment be less desirable than another?"

I closed my trap but quick, and reversed my engines. "It's your money," I told him. I became briskly businesslike. "Do you have any ideas, any angles? Some suggestion as to where I might start?"

He rubbed a thick hand over his knee with satisfaction. Roget was grinning again; even the scarecrow Shulman seemed to relax.

"That is correct, Mr. Knight: we do. We have a theory. Assuming that there are aliens on earth without our knowledge, it becomes obvious that they are deliberately keeping themselves hidden and that they are interested in keeping mankind in ignorance of their existence."

I nodded seriously, humoring him. "That follows."

"Very well, then, it is to be further assumed that they are keeping under surveillance those humans who might possibly suspect their presence on earth."

"And who would they be?" I prompted him cautiously.

"Science fiction fen," Roget blurted. "Half the fen in the country believe there are either aliens on Terra, or that there have been, or will be."

"Fen?" I frowned.

"The plural of fan," Maddigan told me. "We science fiction fen have developed quite a vocabulary of our own."

"Man, men; fan, fen," Roget added.

I suddenly got it. "This club of yours, the—"

"The Scylla Club," Shulman said in his high-pitched voice.

"The Scylla Club. It's a science fiction organization, eh?" Some of my high school mythology came back to me. "Scylla? Wasn't that some six-headed monster Ulysses had trouble with after the Trojan War?"

"That is correct," Maddigan beamed. "The Scylla Club is quite the most exclusive science fiction organization of them all."

It fell into place now. "I see," I told them. "You think that any alien life forms from other worlds would keep their eyes on such groups as yours, since you suspect their presence while practically no one else does. And you want me to investigate the matter."

"That's it," Roget said, grinning with satisfaction and looking like Jimmy Stewart just after he'd killed off all the bad guys in *Destry Rides Again*.

I turned to Maddigan. "All right, I won't pretend that I get this type of case every day, but as I said, it's your money. When did you want me to start?"

"Tomorrow. We would like you to attend a meeting —more of an entertainment, really—of our club tomorrow night. Incognito, of course. After that, we shall consider further steps. Meanwhile, you may busy yourself checking upon any of the aspects of the situation that occur to you."

He gave his belabored right knee one more slap and came to his feet. Shulman and Roget followed, reflecting his satisfaction.

I stuck my pipe in a side pocket and stood up too. "You don't have any special angles except that you think these alien life forms might hang around your science fiction clubs?"

James Maddigan shook his head. "That is why we are hiring your services, Mr. Knight. We trust that you will uncover additional leads."

He took a black pin-seal wallet from an inner coat pocket and fumbled in it, coming out with two twenties and a ten. He laid the bills casually on my desk. "I assume this will be sufficient until we receive your preliminary reports?"

I picked them up just as casually and tossed them into the top drawer. It was the most money I'd had in one lump sum for four months. "Certainly," I said.

They were about to go, but Maddigan hesitated, pursing his heavy lips. "One other matter, Mr. Knight. We would like complete details of your activities; daily written reports, if you will."

That loused up the chances of my bluffing through with this and doing a minimum of leg work and a maximum of sitting comfortably and lazily in the office reading up on the subject in a few books. I groaned inwardly, but on the surface I took it like a man.

I followed them to the door and we went through the formalities again. Maddigan gave me the address of the private home in which the club meeting was to be held the following night, and I noted it down.

"Remember," he said, in the process of leaving, 'most of the club members, and especially their guests, will not be familiar with your identity. We will introduce you as a new fan." He hesitated and considered before adding, "It might be well for you to read a few of the science fiction magazines before tomorrow night. You'll have to be capable of carrying on at least a minimum of pertinent conversation."

"All right, I'll do that," I told him.

After they'd left, I closed the door behind them and leaned against it. "My aching back," I grunted. "Good old Jeb Knight, master mind, the sleuth to end all sleuths."

Something occurred to me. I opened the door again and called down the hall, "Mr. Maddigan!"

He turned pompously, as though not used to being called after. "Yes?"

"Could I borrow that book you were reading from?" I walked down the hall to them as he reached into his coat pocket for it.

"Certainly. Here you are, Mr. Knight. Don't bother to return it; I shall secure another copy."

I returned to the office and to my desk, and sat there a long time before doing anything more than getting the old brier out of my coat and relighting it. The tobacco was stale by now and tasted as if I was burning soft coal, but I didn't have the gumption to get out a fresh pipe and load it.

Finally, I opened the top drawer and took out the two twenties and the ten and looked them over carefully before grunting my acceptance of their genuineness. I put them carefully into my battered wallet and took up the pocket book that Maddigan had given me.

I skimmed through *Life on Other Worlds* for about fifteen minutes, then let it drop again. I wasn't up to wading through the astronomy gobbledygook just at present. Besides, there were a lot of other things to do if I was going to make those detailed reports look authentic enough to keep myself on the payroll of the Scylla Club.

I picked up the phone receiver and dialed the *Daily Chronicle* and asked for editorial. Somebody grumbled, "City desk," and I asked for Marty Rhuling.

A new voice came on after a minute or so. "Rhuling speaking."

"Jeb," I told him, and cut off his flood of amiable insults. "Listen, Marty," I said. "I've got a new job with an awful screwy angle. I thought maybe you could give me a little dope to begin with."

He chortled, "You mean as a private eye? Who is there in this town far enough around the corner to hire *you* after the way you've handled that agency since Lee died?"

"Quiet," I growled. "Don't forget I owe you dough, sadsack."

He pretended sudden meekness. "Fire away with the questions, old comrade-in-arms," he said humbly. "What can I do for you, O debtor of mine?"

"Well, to begin with," I said earnestly, "what and why is a science fiction club?"

CHAPTER TWO

I AWOKE IN THE MORNING from no deep dream of peace, seeing as how I'd spent the evening before at Sam's Bar drinking up the better part of five of the fifty dollars of my retainer fee. I can't remember dreams two minutes after opening my eyes, but I had a vague recollection of green characters scooting around my head in saucer-shaped spaceships. Evidently, no matter what Maddigan's protests, these men from Mars were going to be green to me.

Groaning audibly, I forced myself to sit up and throw my legs over the side of the bed. A shave and a shower helped some. Not much. This was strictly guano for the condors.

I got into shorts, shirt and pants and wobbled my way to the pint-size kitchenette that opens off my combination living and bedroom. Investigation of the aged refrigerator reminded me that I'd forgotten to buy the eggs and ham I was going to treat myself to this morning. There was half a bottle of milk. I tasted it to see if it **was** sour. It wasn't, so I put it on the table and got corn flakes, sugar, a soup plate and a cup and spoon from the cupboard.

I put water on to boil for coffee and then located the powdered coffee extract. In spite of years of trying, and the expense of a dozen different types of foolproof coffee pots, adding a teaspoon of extract to hot water is still the nearest I can get to making a decent cup.

After breakfast, I felt a little better. Not much. I told myself nastily that if I'd had any sense I would have refused the job. If I had, I would have been forced into looking for another way of making a living that much sooner and would have left the detective business to those who knew something about it.

As it was, the fifty bucks was going to let me hang on another week, at least. Well, only until the rent was due. I'd never be able to meet even the pittance charged by the Kroll Building, and that would be the end of *Lee and Knight, Private Investigations.* And good riddance.

I got my shoes and the rest of my clothes on, searched around for my battered felt, finally finding it in the bathroom where I by no means remembered leaving it, and made my way down three flights of squeaking steps to the street.

The brightness of the morning sun had me blinking and squinting. I peered up at the sky in irritation. It was going to be a hot day, plenty hot; lousy weather for a hangover. I walked down Greene Avenue, crossed Seventh Street and entered Tiny's.

Tiny's is one of those wedged in little magazine shops that carry all the publications you've ever heard of and a multitude more. About eleven feet wide, and three times that long, it's crowded between the State Theater, the neighborhood movie house, to the west, and Fred 'n' Beth's Lunch to the east. As you enter, you have thirty feet of magazine racks on your right, beginning with comics and working on down through westerns, love pulps, sport pulps, digest magazines, true detectives, and on into the recesses. On your left you have about ten feet of pocket books, a popcorn outfit, and then the candy and cigarette counter. Halfway down the room, Tiny sits atop a high stool behind the counter. To his left is the cash register; nestled beside it, a box of the king size cigars he smokes and a carton of book matches.

I squeezed myself through eight or ten kids in front of the comic stands. They gave way passively, unnoticingly, and flowed back into their former positions as soon as my passage was complete. Tiny, as usual, was smiling amiably and smoking a cigar that could have been described as half as big as himself without too much exaggeration.

I was still hanging over, but good. "How can a cash customer get through those kids, Tiny?" I grumbled.

An ex-carny midget who'd got tired of being gawked at by the marks and had carefully saved himself enough money to go into business, Tiny didn't actually care whether or not his stand made more than just enough to keep him going. The thing was that it hadn't done him any good; they gawked at him here too. Somehow or other, it seemed to make a difference to him that he wasn't getting paid for it.

He took his cigar from his mouth and grimaced at me. "Jeb," he said, "you owe me a dollar eighty-five for newspapers and mags; none of them kids owe me a red cent. The kind of detective you are, I'll probably never collect the one eighty-five. You can see I'm better off with the kids."

I get it everywhere. Even the newsboys know I couldn't trail an elephant through fresh fallen snow.

I brought out some money and handed him his dollar eighty-five. "All right, here you are," I growled. "You want interest?"

We insulted each other back and forth a while, and then I asked him, "Got any science fiction magazines, Tiny?"

A grimace on Tiny's already impossibly wizened face was something to see. He snorted, "Science fiction mags, yet. There's getting to be as many of them as comics; all over the place, couple new ones start up every month. Since the atom bomb an' the rockets and the flying saucers, everybody's reading science fiction. Not that I mind, of course."

He got down from his stool, came around the end of the counter and led me over to a section of his racks. He waved one of his miniature hands. "There you are, Jeb—science fiction—take your pick."

There must have been a good twenty-five. I ran a hand over my chin and scowled at them. "Which is which?" I asked him.

Tiny hunched up his little shoulders. "They got science fiction mags for everybody, from kids to college perfessors."

He picked one out and handed it to me. "Now this mag is *Planet Stories*. It's pretty strong on action. The guys who read the more serious ones stick their noses up and call it space-opera; you know, wild west stuff. Only the hero isn't a sheriff in Nevada; he's a space-man on Jupiter. It's got a pretty good following, though; one of the oldest mags in the field."

He picked up another. "This here's *Startling Stories*. Guess you could call it the average science fiction mag. It ain't as slick as one or two of the others, but it's for—well, you might say maybe a more advanced reader than *Planet.*"

"All right," I said agreeably. "I'll take those. Which of them would the members of the most exclusive science fiction club read?"

"You mean Scylla?"

I eyed him. "How did you know?"

He waved his cigar airily. "Why, Jeb, I been a fan myself for years. Read 'em all. Wish I had time to be more active. Most of them highbrow fans read *Galaxy, Mag of Fantasy and Science Fiction,* and this here *Astounding.*" He picked up a digest-size magazine and offered it to me. *"Astounding* puts a lot of science in its yarns—the editor and most of the writers are engineers and technicians."

I took up two or three more of the magazines and paid him for the works, saying casually, "Listen, Tiny, what chance do you think there is that the Martians or Venusians have figured out space travel?" I steeled myself, waiting for him to accuse me of being short some marbles. Tiny pulls no punches, especially with his friends.

The little fellow took his cigar from his mouth and pointed it at me seriously. "I'm more inclined to think they're from Alpha Centauri or some other nearby star."

I blinked at him. "Who?" I asked.

He said impatiently, "The aliens. I don't think they're from Mars or Venus; I think they're from some other solar system. But I'm willing to argue about it. What makes you think they're from Mars?"

I stared at him for a long moment, wondering whether he was ribbing me. His wizened little face is so wrinkled that half the time you can't make out his expression. "Let's drop that part of it," I told him finally. "What makes you think there are aliens here on earth?"

He hunched his thin shoulders impatiently. "Anybody could tell you that—anybody with half a brain who'd done any looking into the matter. What do you think these flying saucers are?"

Tiny wasn't kidding. The wrinkled little runt was dead serious.

I said, "Listen, Tiny, I'll see you later. We'll talk about it then. I don't know enough now to have any opinions."

He walked off to wait on another customer. "Okay," he told me over his shoulder, "it was you who brung it up."

CHAPTER THREE

I GOT OUT to the Scylla Club affair about an hour or so after it was scheduled to begin, wanting to be sure that Maddigan, or at least Shulman or Roget, was there before I made my appearance.

The house was situated in an outlying section of town known as Brentwood after old Thomas W. Brent, our fair city's first multi-millionaire, who had made his dough back when millionaires did it the hard way. Brentwood was still in there pitching, but it had really been tops thirty or so years ago. The heavy moola crowd had moved further out; the almost-rich were left behind.

The Brentwood streetcar had taken me down East First Street to Gates Avenue; from there I walked over to number 404. It wasn't one of those gigantic old relics—mansions, they called them—but it was larger than the average family lives in any more. It looked as though it had eight or nine rooms, probably three baths; a half-acre of lawn stretched out before and a tremendous hedge walled garden occupied the rear. There were only two other houses in the block. As I sauntered up the neatly graveled walk to the door, I could hear the noises of the party coming from the garden.

A big, clean cut, easygoing-looking guy of about thirty came to the door a minute or so after I rang. He was wearing a "West Coast type sport coat, slacks and heavy sport shoes. You don't see jackets that loud this far East. On him it looked fine. He had a smile of welcome as he opened up, but it faded when he saw that he didn't recognize me. He waited for me to say something.

I didn't know if he was in on the deal or not. I said, "I'm a friend of Jim Maddigan's. This is where the Scylla Club meeting is being held, isn't it?" I was assuming that even a pompous stuffed shirt gets James shortened to Jim among his friends.

The smile came back—he looked better that way— and he held out his hand. There was a heavy gold ring on one finger. "I'm Ross Maddigan." There was genuine warmth in his voice. "Come on in. What was your name?"

I shook the hand; he had a firm, dry clasp. "Knight," I told him, "Jeb Knight."

"Jeb, like in Jeb Stuart, the Confederate general?" He led me back into the house, taking my hat and tossing it absently to the top of a pile on a hall table.

"The middle name is Custer," I confessed. "One grandfather was in the Northern cavalry, the other in the Southern."

A library opened off to one side of us, a large living room to the other. The hall stretched back into the rear where all the guests seemed to be congregated. The place was well done but carelessly kept up. I got the impression that Ross Maddigan didn't give a hoot about the mundane things—at least so long as he had a hundred thousand or so in the bank.

I followed him down the hall. He said, "How could the Northern one stand the fact that your first name is Jeb?"

"He didn't know it. Whenever he was visiting, the family called me Custer. We didn't want to start the war over again."

Ross Maddigan pushed open a swinging door and we entered a large kitchen. He motioned vaguely at cupboards, a tremendous refrigerator and a laden table, saying, "I never serve things at one of these Scylla Club brawls. Science fiction fen are the most informal characters you've ever met. I just load up the icebox with cold cuts and odds and ends, put the liquor out on the kitchen table, and everybody makes their own. You do the same, Jeb." He reached for a glass. "You can't make spaghetti sauce, can you?"

"No," I told him.

He said, pointlessly as far as I was concerned, "Stan Mullen isn't going to be here tonight."

Two of the party, a couple of earnest-looking youngsters in their early twenties, were mixing themselves drinks and squabbling over somebody named Bradbury. All I caught was one of them insisting that his stories were good but they weren't science fiction. The other one let him know he was crazy. They were both deadly serious about it.

"What'll you have, Jeb?" Ross Maddigan asked me. "Bourbon, rye, Irish, Scotch, applejack . . ."

My eyebrows went up. "Apple? Where'd you pick it up? I haven't seen any apple for years."

"You can get it," he said. "I used to drink it up in the Catskills before repeal; this store-boughten stuff isn't as good." He picked up the bottle and frowned at it. "It's bonded," he complained, "but somehow it doesn't *taste* aged."

I had some applejack with ginger ale and a twist of lemon. Nobody seems to know it any more, but it makes one of the best

highballs you can wrap yourself around. I gave an inward sigh for
yesteryear.

Ross mixed himself a drink, too, and we started working on
them. The others left, still squabbling about Bradbury.

"I suppose you're a relative of Jim Maddigan's," I said, taking
the time now to size him up over the rim of my glass. He was in
his early thirties, nearly six feet tall and was probably pushing two
hundred, although you had to look twice to notice it. He carried his
weight easily, caring no more about it than he did about his already receding hairline. Ross Maddigan took life easily, and he
liked living it.

"Nephew," he answered, and somehow I got the impression
that he and his uncle weren't particularly close. "How long have
you been a fan, Jeb?"

I had to watch myself here. "Not very long," I told him. "Got
interested when atom bombs and rockets started doing things the
science fiction magazines have been predicting for the past twenty
years." I wondered if twenty years was the correct figure.

"Ummm," he said, jerking his head slightly in amused memory.
"We've got a member of Scylla—a writer— who did up a story
back in 1944 and sent it to one of the magazines. They day after
the issue hit the stands two F.B.I, men came around—real tough,
understand—and wanted to know who on the Manhattan Project
had been shooting off his mouth. Hell, Cleve had never even heard
of the Manhattan Project; he didn't know what they were talking
about."

"Well, where'd he get the dope?" I asked.

Ross Maddigan stirred his shoulders and grinned. "Science fiction writers, just as you said, have been writing about the atom
bomb for the past twenty years and more. Cleve just happened to
pick an embarrassing time to write his story. Hiroshima came a
few months later."

A girl wearing swash horn-rimmed glasses came wandering in,
empty tumbler in her hand. "I'm beginning to feel ignored," she
said with mock petulance.

She was somewhere short of twenty-five, with blue eyes, less
than spectacular brownish hair and a figure it was hard to take
your eyes from. She was probably medium-sized, but constructed
so neatly that she seemed small. Her face was oval and the skin
drawn a shade too tightly over the bone underneath, putting faint
hollows under her cheekbones. Her lips were on the thick side,
giving her somewhat of a sulky look. One eyebrow had a way of

twitching slightly when she spoke, which did something to you that another woman couldn't have accomplished with everything she had.

She saw that she didn't know me and her eyebrows went up questioningly.

The doorbell was ringing. Ross Maddigan said, "Sorry, darling, I'll have more time after everybody gets here." He looked a little harassed. "Julie Sharp—Jeb Knight. See you both later," he finished over his shoulder, and bustled back toward the front door.

I felt like saying, "Well, helloooo," in that tone of voice, and when our eyes met, she knew it. Her eyes had just a faint hint of violet in the blue, and there was a cautious dusting of freckles across the bridge of her nose.

"I don't believe I've seen you around before," she said conversationally.

"I'm new to fandom," I told her, clearing the lump that had come up into my throat with a quick slug of the highball.

She smiled, boasting even white teeth and bringing attention to the fact that her lips needed only the faintest touch of red to show them to the best advantage. "So am I," she admitted. "Sometimes I think I come around just for the laughs. Heavens, how can you people get so serious about it? Time travel, trips to the moon, interplanetary warfare; sometimes I wonder how anyone like—well, say Jim, can get worked up about such things."

I was supposed to be one of them, so I said, "Some people go nuts about historical fiction. I think it shows more awareness to be interested in the future, especially in these times." That sounded like a plausible answer; maybe a bit stuffy, but plausible.

She let me mix her another drink, Scotch and water, and when I'd finished it she took the glass and said, "Well, here's to the Bems."

"Yeah," I answered vaguely, and took a gulp of my applejack. I wondered what a Bem was.

Her eyes narrowed almost imperceptibly and she started to say something just as Harold Shulman, his clothes as baggy as ever, and his eyes blinking rapidly behind his heavy-lensed specs, rambled into the kitchen from the garden.

"Here you are," he said shrilly, sounding as though I should be somewhere else.

"Hello, there, Harry," I said, assuming that we were supposedly old friends. I wished that the three of them had briefed me more on just what sort of a game I was supposed to play. For all I knew, part of my job was to suspect Julie Sharp of being a visitor from Venus. As far as that went, for my money she was Venus herself. Shulman would have done me a big favor by staying away for another five or ten minutes.

"Hi, Miss Sharp," he said; then, "You getting acquainted, Jeb? Maybe I better introduce you around."

Julie told him hello, and I sighed inwardly and said, "All right; wait until I get another drink." I had a sneaking suspicion that Julie Sharp was the only person at the party that I really cared about meeting and that I could stand a degree of fortifying.

I got my drink, said half a dozen words to Julie to the effect that I was looking forward to seeing her again, and was hauled off by the gangling Shulman. Her eyes laughed after me and I got the feeling that I wasn't kidding her.

Harry Shulman ushered me into the garden, whispering in a conspirator's voice, "Discover anything yet?"

I looked at him plaintively. "Listen, I've only been here ten minutes. What did you expect, a flock of handcuffed Martians??"

He didn't recognize the sarcasm. He had me by the arm and was leading me to a semi-quiet corner of the garden back toward the rear, near the hedge. "I thought you wanted to introduce me around," I said.

"I'll do that shortly," he told me, trying to keep his shrill voice low. "First, I wanted to show you something."

Well, the liquor was good, at least *one* of the girls was better, and I had an idea that the overgrown refrigerator would be full of the kind of food I haven't been able to afford for many a moon. Who was I to complain when I was getting paid for that kind of treatment?

He led me to the shady cover of an old tree, well away from the nearest group of wrangling fans. There was a heavy wooden bench beneath the low branches, and we sat down. He brought a fold of mimeographed and stapled papers from an inner pocket. "I wanted to show you this," he said.

"All right, what is it?"

He handed it to me. "It's my fanzine," he said shrilly. "You're an outsider and I'd like your unbiased opinion."

Here we went again.

"What's a fanzine?" I asked, holding it up so I could see it in the dim light. The cover sported a semi-nude girl, standing in front of what I supposed was a spaceship.

He explained while I thumbed through it. "In science fiction you have prozines and fanzines. The prozines—professional magazines—are the regular commercial publications like *Imagination* and *Super-Science* and *Fantastic Adventures.*"

I cued him, "And the fanzines?"

"Well," he pointed at the sheaf of mimeographed pages I held, 'that's a typical fanzine. Most fen would like to write themselves, but since they can't make the grade in the prozines—not at first, at least—they put out these fanzines and print each other's stories, articles and art work."

I looked at it with more interest. "You mean the science fiction fans go to all the trouble to put these things together just for a hobby?"

He was indignant. "You should see some of them. Some of the fen can afford to print or planograph theirs. You should see Bob Tucker's *Science Fiction News Letter.*"

I got back to the point. "All right, what did you want me to do with this?"

He blinked at me earnestly. "Well, part of your job involves finding out all about fandom, and fanzines are a major part of fandom. I thought you might as well get your impression of the fanzines from my *Off-Trail Fantasy* as any. I'd like to have your opinion of some of the stories. There's one in particular that I did myself called *Ultimate Destiny.*

There was a wistful note in his high voice.

"All right," I said, folding it lengthwise and putting it into an inner pocket. "I'll read it."

"Don't you want to read it now?" he asked, blinking again.

"Listen, Harry," I said, noting my glass was empty, "you hired me to check on whether or not any extraterrestrials—" I'd picked up that word in the stories I'd been reading all afternoon—"were hanging around your affairs. I don't think sitting here reading your magazine is going to get me very far along in that direction."

He began to say something, but didn't. Instead, he thought a minute. Finally, "Well, let me know what you think when you *do* finish it."

"All right," I told him agreeably. I got to my feet. "Now do you have any ideas on where I should begin checking on your aliens?"

Harry Shulman moved the thin shoulders inside his ill-fitting coat, still looking disappointed. "I'll introduce you to some of the others," he said. "I guess it will have to be up to you to think of some angle."

For the next fifteen minutes, I was taken from one group to another, being introduced around. James Maddigan had said that most of those present wouldn't know my purpose; from what I could see, none of them did. Among others, Shulman introduced me to Art Roget, both of them pretending that Roget and I hadn't met before. I didn't get it, but it was all right with me.

Maddigan—the older Maddigan—was in one of the groups too. He said hello cheerfully enough, but made no particular indication that we were acquainted. For my dough, they weren't handling it very well. James Maddigan, according to the story I'd told his nephew, was supposedly my friend and sponsor in science fiction circles.

But it wasn't my money. Why should I care how they wasted it?

Shulman drifted away after a while and I stopped with one group long enough to get involved in an argument about a writer named Kuttner. I was on fairly firm ground, since I remembered reading one of his stories that afternoon. I held my own.

Later—several drinks later—I found myself in a circle discussing whether or not pen-names should be used by authors. It turned out that some of the science fiction writers—Kuttner among them—had a half dozen or more pseudonyms. One group of the debaters was of the opinion that this was fine; the other wanted a writer to have just one by-line even though several of his stories appeared in the same issue of a magazine. I couldn't see that it made much difference and made the mistake of saying so; both sides teamed up to give me the oatmeal look. I wandered off for another drink and maybe a snack from the kitchen. Besides, I wondered where Julie Sharp was.

She wasn't in the kitchen. James Maddigan was. He stood to one side of the table which held the liquor supplies, arguing with a slightly plumpish, ultra-sophisticated-looking blonde, who was as out of place at this party as an icicle on the hot side of Mercury.

She must have been a bit older than Julie Sharp— probably pushing thirty. Hollywood might have said, *Jean Harlow type,* and left it there, and been pretty accurate, too. Her looks were half God-given, half store-boughten; but on her you didn't mind. She had a wide mouth, full kissable lips, and a nice nose which you didn't see too much of since your eyes continually came back to that full mouth. Her eyes were hard to explain; somehow you got the feeling that something was missing in them, a something that once was called breeding.

Maddigan knocked it off when I entered, but he was still frowning when he said, "Sandra, may I present Mr. Knight, a newcomer to fandom? Jeb, my wife."

So not even his wife was in on my identity. Perhaps he suspected her of being from Saturn or some such. She must have been at least fifteen years younger than he, and by the manner in which she let her eyes run up and down me, the difference in years was beginning to tell in their home life.

We went through the formalities, and her hand was just a touch suggestive, stayed just a fraction too long in mine.

I said, by way of making conversation, "Have you been a fan long, Mrs. Maddigan?"

She pouted—prettily—but I hate women who pout. "I'm not a fan," she admitted. "I just come to keep tabs on Jim." It was probably meant to be humorous, but I had a feeling that the checking was going the other way.

Maddigan puffed out his heavy lips and said, "How are you progressing, Jeb?"

I let my right shoulder rise and drop. "Still at the stage of getting my bearings," I told him. Actually, I was at the stage of getting good and tight.

"Don't forget the detailed reports," he said, waggling a thick finger at me. "Very important."

"All right," I said agreeably. I wondered what the devil he expected to find in a report; possibly some account of my trailing a Martian up and down the city in taxicabs.

"*What* report?" Sandra wanted to know. There was a faint suspicion in her voice and in her narrowed eyes.

He covered admirably. "Mr. Knight, my dear, is checking up on some real estate for me."

So that was his line: real estate. At least the Scylla Club boasted variety. Harry Shulman had introduced me to editors and publishers, and a half-dozen doctors of this and that; mingled with them had been a dozen or so clerks and housewives, a half-dozen students and even a ship's officer. Science fiction evidently wasn't confined to one stratum of society, one age, or one sex. As a matter of fact, Maddigan alone seemed out of place, actually; a stuffed shirt of a businessman in surroundings that before yesterday I'd have thought were suitable only to inmates of nut factories.

Most of those I'd met seemed considerably above average in perception and education. I'd given up wondering why they'd selected time travel and trips to Mars as their hobby when there were things like wine, women and whistling running around loose.

We were tossing light bits of conversation back and forth, but there was still a tension between Maddigan and his frau, and I began looking for an excuse to cut it off and wander elsewhere. Besides that, I still wanted to locate Julie again.

I opened my mouth to say something just as Art Roget came in. His Jimmy Stewart grin was conspicuously gone; his face reflected shock and disbelief, and he stumbled awkwardly over the doorstep as he entered. You didn't need intuition to know something was wrong.

He muttered, as though to himself, "I've got to call an ambulance. Harry's dead; he's squashed all over, like he fell from a tall building. I've got to call the police—or somebody." He made his way past us and into the hallway, looking for the phone.

It took a full minute to put together what he'd said. In spite of the expression on Roget's face, my first impression was that it must be a gag. But there was a loud, agitated hum, rapidly increasing in volume, emanating from the garden.

Maddigan was the first to speak. He said, "Squashed all over? That's nonsense; the highest building in this vicinity isn't more than three stories."

CHAPTER FOUR

IT WAS NONSENSE, all right. Utterly impossible, but there it was. What had been Harry Shulman, a shrill-voiced, nervous little guy who took his science fiction seriously, was now a flattened, gory mess rivaling anything I'd seen in the war.

He was less than a dozen feet from the bench where we had sat talking about his fanzine, or whatever he called it, perhaps an hour or so earlier. Face down on the ground, the best description I could give would be to repeat what Art Roget had said—"He's squashed all over, like he fell from a tall building." I doubted that there was a whole bone left in his body.

I turned my face away as quickly as the next one.

James Maddigan was standing behind me, his eyes popping and his jowls quivering. He opened his mouth a couple of times as though to blubber something, but closed it again. I headed back toward the house and he followed me.

The club members were milling around like a mob without a leader, several of them semi-hysterical. One girl stood in the middle of the garden swaying, her hands held to her stomach, her mouth open and stupid with shock and with whimpering noises coming from it. I could hear someone else being sick behind a lilac bush. Three or four of the guests had taken one look at the body and had made a beeline for the house, probably—bound for their hats and the front door. Sandra led them.

James Maddigan blurted, "Shouldn't you take over, Knight? Shouldn't you attempt to . . ."

We had regained the kitchen by now. The wonderful bun I'd been building all evening was gone. I reached for the bottle of applejack and gurgled a stiff drink into a dirty glass sitting there on the kitchen table, not taking the time to locate a clean one.

"Why me?" I growled at Maddigan. "Didn't your pal Roget phone the police? They'll be taking over soon enough."

"But shouldn't someone," he motioned nervously with his head toward the garden, "tell them not to touch the body, or whatever it is you tell them until the police arrive?"

"All right," I said. I took another deep swallow. "It's all right with me. You tell them. Not that anybody's going to touch *that* body."

"Yes, but you're a detective; you know the procedure." He was staring at me as though I were out of my mind. His overbearing pomposity was gone.

I glowered back. "Why? Do I look like Philip Marlowe or Michael Shane? I've never seen a murder before in my life."

"Murder?" His eyes blinked rapidly, for a brief moment reminding me of young Shulman who wasn't going to be doing any blinking ever again.

I finished the applejack and poured another; the first hadn't done me much good. "Listen, make up your mind," I told him impatiently. "First you get all excited about not touching the body, and about getting the police, and preventing everybody from leaving; now you're shocked because I mention the word murder."

He blinked again. "I suppose you are correct. I knew it from the first, but *murder* . . . Perhaps he fell from the tree."

I snorted. "Yeah. But anybody that got *that* splattered from falling out of a tree must have been climbing a redwood, not an oak, or whatever that is out there."

"Well—still, someone should tell them they must not leave until the police arrive."

"All right," I said placatingly, "let's go. You go out into the garden and tell them; I'll go into the hall where the coats and hats are."

The sirens started screaming a few minutes later, and the next half-hour was principally a madhouse of arriving cops, homicide detail men, ambulance and medical examiners.

I cornered the rest of the fifth of applejack and went back into the garden and found a bench as far away from the remains of Harry Shulman as I could. The apple didn't do me much good, but I worked away at it carefully and didn't think about anything at all until a patrolman came to get me.

He said, "You been inside to talk to the lieutenant yet?"

I came to my feet and sat the nearly empty bottle down on the ground. "No," I admitted. "Let's go." There was warm moisture in my palms.

A couple of uniformed officers, one of them taking shorthand notes, and two plainclothesmen were in the living room. They looked tired.

The patrolman who'd rounded me up said, "This is Lieutenant Philip Davis; he's in charge," and left the room again.

Davis looked up at me from where he sat on a heavy leather couch. "Where've I seen you before, eh?" He stared at me out of a pair of cold pale eyes set close to a narrow nose. His skin stretched tight over his face, and you got the impression that he needed lots of good food and lots of sunshine, but that he probably wasn't interested in acquiring either. He was small, belligerent and feisty.

I didn't remember ever having seen the patrolman who was taking the shorthand, but he looked up and said, "It's Jeb Knight, Lieutenant; Lee and Knight. He used to be Ken Lee's partner."

Lieutenant Davis shot a quick glance at me, as though seeing me for the first time. His rasping voice didn't go with his small body. He sneered, "Oh, yeah. Jeb Knight, special investigator. You're the genius who handled that Holliday matter, eh? How come you've still got a license? Or have you?"

I'd been expecting this. I wished that I'd had better results from the fifth of applejack in the garden. I said, "Yes, I've still got my license."

Davis snorted, "Why the devil did Ken Lee ever pick you for a partner, eh? Lee was a pretty good man."

I said, "We knew each other during the war, Lieutenant."

The detective lieutenant crossed his legs, revealing overly pale skin above a garterless sock. He said, less nastily now, "Why you stick in the detective racket with no more on the ball than you have I don't know, but that's your business."

"Yeah," I said tonelessly.

He shot another of his quick glances at me, to see if I was being sarcastic. He said, "I've had about twenty of this gang in here already and I haven't got enough out of them even to begin with. Maybe you can do me some good, eh?" His tone of voice suggested that he wasn't very hopeful.

"I'll do what I can, Lieutenant. I'm afraid it's not much."

"Well, first of all, what are you doing here?"

Here it came. "I'm on a case," I told him. "Three of these people hired me yesterday for an investigation."

"Get this down, Roberts, eh?" Davis said to the cop who had recognized me. "What three?"

"James Maddigan, Arthur Roget and Harold Shulman," I said, and half closed my eyes in anticipation of the blast.

"Harold Shulman! You mean that stiff out there is a client of yours?"

The other detective laughed nastily. "Oh, brother; anybody that hires this character ought to take out life insurance." He was a beefy cop, with thick neck and shoulders and a red, perpetually grinning face. His eyes were big and they popped.

"Shut up, Mike," Davis snapped. "What were you investigating for them?" he growled to me.

I took a deep breath; this was it. "They hired me to investigate the presence of space travelers on earth."

There was a pregnant silence. Only three of them had been listening to me, but now the other patrolman looked up and said, "I thought he said . . ."

Davis said softly, "He did. Evidently we've got a wise guy here, eh? He's been reading about how private eyes make monkeys out of the police force. He wants to make like Sam Spade."

I held up the palms of my hands. "You asked me. I told you. Maddigan, Roget and Shulman came to my office yesterday afternoon. They gave me a long song and dance about being suspicious of alien life forms here on earth. They wanted me to check up at their club meetings."

"Go on," Davis rasped; "keep on cracking wise. You'll wind up the night in a cell."

"So help me, Lieutenant," I told him desperately. "They figured if there were any aliens from space—that's the way they put it— on earth secretly, that they'd be hanging around the science fiction clubs checking to see that nobody got on to them."

Without taking his pale eyes from me, Davis took a small bottle from his vest pocket, unscrewed the top and shook out a pill. He said finally, "Mike, go get this Maddigan and Roget. On your way back, bring me a glass of water, eh?"

Mike left. Davis leaned back and brooded at me with empty eyes. "How well did you know this Shulman?" he asked.

"Not until yesterday."

"What killed him?"

"You know better than I do. What did the deputy coroner think?"

"None of your business. What did *you* think, eh?"

Nobody had asked me, but I was rapidly getting the impression that this was going to last for a while, so I pulled up a straight-backed chair and sat down, reaching into my coat pocket for pipe and tobacco.

I said, "He looked to me as though he'd fallen from a great height."

He fingered his pill. "How great? Don't light that damn pipe. It's thick enough in here already."

The air in the big living room was perfectly all right, as far as I could notice, but I stuck the pipe back into my pocket. "I don't know," I said. "I saw a guy in France once whose parachute didn't open; he looked quite a bit like Shulman does."

The detective named Mike came in again with the glass of water. "The other two are outside, Lieutenant."

Davis took the glass of water, popped the pill into his mouth and emptied the water down over it. He said, "Okay, Mike, show them in." He looked back at me. "You suggesting that he fell from an airplane, eh?"

I rubbed the sweat in my left palm with my right thumb and shook my head. "No. I just said that he looked the same as . . ."

He cut me off as Maddigan and Roget entered. Maddigan's jowls were still quivering and Roget didn't look as though he'd ever regain that grin of his. Their eyes went nervously all about the room, coming back finally to rest on me.

Davis growled, "You didn't tell me earlier that you'd hired Jeb Knight, here."

Neither of them answered him; but for that matter, it hadn't exactly been worded as a question.

Davis said, "Evidently, Knight has some reason for attempting to hide the purpose of you three—counting Shulman—going to his office yesterday. I shouldn't have to tell you that this is homicide, murder. And when murder comes along . . ."

Maddigan said nervously, "You don't understand. We don't mind at all telling you about it; we just didn't think it was important."

Roget said, "No, sir." He looked like a grammar school kid up before the principal.

Davis' voice hardened. "Leave it to us to decide what's important and what isn't, eh? What was wise-guy Knight hired for?"

"To investigate the presence of alien life forms on Terra."

There was silence again.

Davis said finally, "Mike, get me another glass of water, eh?" He ran his eyes over Maddigan and Roget, giving them a thorough appraisal. "You *look* halfway intelligent," he muttered, "but you must be off your rockers or you wouldn't waste your money on Knight, no matter what you wanted investigated. Now give me the whole story, eh?"

Roget said hesitantly, "It all started because of the Convention, the AnnCon. We're on the entertainment committee."

Lieutenant Davis slowly took the bottle from his vest pocket again and shook two pills into his hand. He said softly, "I continually get the impression that I came into this conversation late; either that, or you guys are ribbing me." His voice suddenly became sharper. "I hate wise guys," he rasped. "Start making sense, dammit."

Maddigan took over. "The tenth anniversary of the first World Science Fiction Convention is to be held here in this city in a few days, Lieutenant. We call it the AnnCon as an abbreviation of Anniversary Convention. The Eighth Convention, held in the Northwest, we called the NorWesCon; the one in New Orleans, Louisiana, was the NolaCon, and . . ."

"Okay, okay, so you're going to have a convention here; so what?"

Maddigan was flustered, but he went on, "As Art just said, he and I—and Shulman—were on the entertainment committee. We wanted to have something different, some skit—well, not exactly a skit—but something with a stf. . . ."

"Eh?" Davis scowled.

"A stf. Scientifiction abbreviated. We wanted something different. Well, we thought that for only fifty or seventy-five dollars we could hire a private detective to investigate the presence of aliens from space here on earth. We'd have him do up daily reports and then we'd read the reports before the convention. We thought that if we were able to convince him we were sincere, he'd make a serious attempt to do that for which we hired him." Maddigan ended lamely, "We thought it would provide considerable amusement at the convention, reading his reports."

Davis said, still unbelievingly, "Well, why'd you hire a jerk like Knight, eh? Why didn't you get a decent agency? Didn't you read about him in the papers last month?"

Art Roget shot an embarrassed look at me. "We were afraid that the larger agencies wouldn't take the assignment."

I flinched, probably noticeably.

The plainclothesman named Mike had returned with the water. Now he started to laugh. "Oh, brother. What he means is, he didn't think anybody but a sap like Buster, here, would take on such a case!"

Even Davis grinned sourly. "Shut up, Mike," he growled. "This isn't getting us anywhere." He went back to Maddigan. "Okay. So you hired Jeb Knight to check up on whether or not there were any Martians here on earth, just for the gag, eh? What was he doing here tonight? Never mind, I get it. This was where the investigation started, eh? And he hardly got here before this Shulman kid was found dead."

He rubbed his chin reflectively. "Who was the last person you saw with young Shulman, Roget?"

The eyes of both Roget and Maddigan went to me.

"Oh, for Pete's sake," I protested, "I hadn't been around him for more than an hour."

Roget said, "The last I saw Harry, he was taking Mr. Knight around introducing him to the different members."

Maddigan cleared his throat uncomfortably. He looked at me with more or less apology, as though that did any good. "That is correct," he said. "I am afraid that I must report the same. The last time I saw Harry, he brought Mr. Knight to a small group of us who were discussing whether or not Kuttner predominated in his collaboration stories with his wife."

Lieutenant Davis came to his feet and walked around behind the couch. He leaned down, placing his elbows on its back and turned his gray eyes on me thoughtfully.

"Knight," he said, "I've been wondering about you ever since that Holliday case. What kind of a discharge did you get from the army, eh?"

"Not a medical one," I snapped irritably.

CHAPTER FIVE

I GOT HOME late that night, very late; but I was at the office at my usual time in the morning. I hadn't slept much. I'd felt cold sober by the time I got home, but morning greeted me with a skull-cracking hangover anyway. It started in at about five o'clock, and at six-thirty I gave up any thoughts of further sleep and groaned my way out of bed.

All the endless questions on the part of Detective Lieutenant Davis and his boys hadn't brought out much the night before—not that I knew of, at least. As far as anyone had seemed able to remember, I was the last person seen with Harry Shulman, and that had been an hour before he was found dead. It might even have been more; at that type of party it's hard to keep track of the passage of time.

I hadn't heard the coroner's report, but I had no doubt about the cause of death. It might have been faked—possibly—but I would have laid my bottom dollar that Harry Shulman had fallen from a tremendous height to his death.

Unwilling to risk anything more than coffee on my stomach, I was out of the apartment by seven-thirty and five minutes later into Tiny's for the morning papers. It was early, but there were already two early-bird kids at the comic stands seriously studying the latest exploits of *Sheena, the Jungle Girl*. I caught up the papers and brushed past them to where Tiny sat on his stool, monarch of all he surveyed. He leered at me when he saw me come in; he'd obviously been at the papers already.

"Shut up," I said, before he could get a dig into me.

He took the cigar from his mouth. "Sure, Jeb," he said, ignoring my demand, "but why don't you drop out of the private eye game and get a job as a—well, as a matter of fact, off hand I can't think of *anything* you could do." His wizened face grinned, monkey-like, at me; he was having the time of his life.

"Shut up," I told him again, handed him the money for the papers and left. The kids swayed unconsciously out of my way as I approached and swayed back as soon as I was by.

At the corner of Herkimer and Greene, I waited momentarily as the proprietor of Ted's Dispensary opened his front door. I followed him in and bought myself a fifth of fifth rate whiskey. He said something about the weather and I agreed it *was* going to be hot again. Evidently he hadn't read the papers yet; at least I got no cracks from him.

I crossed the street and waited for a bus to take me down to City Center. Three passed before a driver decided there was even enough standing room to let me on.

Fifteen minutes later found me unlocking the door of *Lee and Knight, Private Investigations.* I entered, put the bottle on the desk with the newspapers, and tossed my hat to the coat rack. I went around behind the desk and sank into my swivel chair, allowing myself a faint groan.

I could feel something uncomfortable bulging in my inner coat pocket, and pulled it out. It was *Off Trail Fantasy,* Harry Shulman's amateur magazine. I'd forgotten about having it. I grunted and tossed it into the desk's second drawer which is reserved for things that some day I want to take another look at . . .

I sat there a while, staring up at the framed license on the wall, the document that stated that Lee and Knight were detectives.

That's what *it* said.

I took up the first of the three papers I'd bought. They were having at me again in great style, but great. The *News* wanted me thrown into the cooler; the *Tribune* was more conservative: all they wanted was my license revoked. The *Chronicle* mentioned casually that in the old days—the tone of the editorial suggested that they were the good old days—an aroused citizenry would have escorted me to the city's limits on a rail and garbed in the latest in tar and feathers sportwear. All three of the rags devoted more space to me than they did to the killing. That was the angle they latched onto—the dead boy was a client of mine—they rehashed the Holliday case, happily.

To my moderate surprise, the science fiction angle was left out of it. The Scylla Club was mentioned, but none of the papers went into a description of the nature of the outfit. Not that it was of any interest to me.

I got up and got myself the glass that stands on the wash bowl behind the screen. It was dirty, so I gave it a quick rinse and brought it back to the desk, reaching for the bottle.

A shadow fell on the opaque glass of the hall door.

I stashed the bottle and glass away into the large bottom drawer and said, "Come in," almost before the knock sounded.

It was Ross Maddigan, a worried frown on his open face instead of the easy friendliness of the night before. His coat and pants still didn't match, but the jacket wasn't quite as loud as the one he'd been wearing the last time I'd seen him.

"Hello, Ross," I said, sticking out my hand. "Come on in."

He shook the hand, looked around for a chair, found one and slumped down into it, holding his hat by its rim with both hands. I walked around behind the desk and got seated myself.

I figured it was his turn to talk; he hadn't said anything yet. Finally he made a face and looked up at me. I just sat there. He tossed his hat to the desk and rubbed the back of his head with his right hand. His face had ruefulness on it.

He said, "You didn't tell me you were a detective last night."

"Private detective," I told him. "It was part of the game, evidently, for nobody to know at first."

"What game?"

"I thought you knew by now. Your uncle, and Roget and Shulman, hired me for a gag they wanted to put on at some convention."

"The AnnCon?"

"I guess that was it. Anyway, the idea was for me to investigate the possibility of extra-terrestrials hanging around your club meetings. They were going to read the reports I made on my progress before the convention."

Some of the worry left his face momentarily, but he didn't quite get to the smiling point. "It would have made a pretty good gag," he said absently.

"I guess so. It's easier for the next guy to get it than it is for me. For me it wasn't so funny."

He hadn't heard that, I suppose. He said slowly, "What happened last night, Jeb?"

My eyebrows went up. "Harry Shulman was killed."

"It coudn't possibly have been an accident?" He said that very slowly.

I shook my head. "I don't know what the medical examiner's report was, but from the looks of that body, it couldn't have been an accident."

"Why?"

"He looked as though every bone in his body was broken, but there he was beneath the branches of that tree. He'd died somewhere else and was moved to that spot."

I anticipated his next question and beat him to it. "He was too broken up to have died merely from falling from the tree. Besides, there would have been signs of his fall; broken branches, twigs, and so forth."

He said suddenly, "I want you to investigate it, Jeb."

"Who, me?" I stared at him unbelievingly.

He didn't say anything, so I laughed, with a touch of bitterness, and added, "Listen, Ross, the police are investigating Shulman's death and they're doing it a damn sight better than *any* private operator could, not to speak of doing it better than *I* could."

Ross Maddigan shook his head earnestly. "I know the record of the police department on homicide cases. Less than half of them are solved in this city. Harry Shulman was a friend of mine; besides that, he was a guest at my home when—"

I shook my head at him negatively. "Listen, Ross," I said, "you've got the wrong idea. In the first place, you've picked up the belief that private detectives solve murders and that police departments don't. You're wrong on both counts. Private detectives very seldom, if ever, get tied up in homicide cases. You're right in thinking that a lot of murders are never solved, but the kind you're thinking about are usually the gang killings and such. This personal type of homicide is almost always cleared up by the police."

He wasn't convinced.

"Listen," I said. "They've got the facilities, the manpower, the laboratories, the resources, to do these things right. All I am is one private detective and not a very good one at that. Don't you ever read the papers? Get a load of the panning I take."

"Yes," he argued, "but you were on the scene and—"

"And still don't know what's going on," I finished for him. "Hell, Ross, even if I wanted to work on this for you, I couldn't. The police wouldn't let me. They don't want private investigators messing around in homicide cases, and what's more, they won't stand for it."

He rubbed his chin with the back of his hand ruefully. "I guess you're right. I must be too worked up about this; but every time I think of Harry lying there under that tree—"

"Yeah," I said, thinking of offering him a drink, but deciding it was too early for decent people to be drinking. I came to my feet suggestively; and he picked up his hat from the desk and followed my lead. I led him to the door. Ross Maddigan was a nice enough guy, and I didn't mind talking to him, but I wanted to get back to my bottle. "Thanks, anyway, for thinking of me," I said, hitting him lightly on the shoulder in a spurt of camaraderie. "It was a pleasure to meet you last night— even if the evening did wind up in tragedy." I told myself I sounded as though I were making a speech.

"Yeah, sure, Jeb," he said. "Well, so long."

"So long, Ross," I told him.

After he'd gone, I went back to my desk and opened the bottom drawer and reached for the bottle. My throbbing head wasn't getting any better, and what I needed was the whole pelt of the hound that had bit me the night before.

The bottle had a cork in it. I swore inwardly and reached for my pocket knife. I was in no mood for jockeying with corks, so the process of digging it out, piece by piece, took longer than ordinarily. I finally wound up by pushing the tail end of it down into the bottle, but at least I was to the whiskey.

I reached for my glass, and a voice said lightly, "Rather early for it, isn't it?"

I shot a startled look upward at her.

She stood there, pouting in a mocking way, and looking somewhat thinner than she had the night before. Her blouse was a simple and severe white, under a darkish blue suit which fitted her lines lovingly. Her narrow, well-bred feet sported patent-leather pumps; above them, her nylons emphasized the long slim ankles, the beautiful calves. She looked very edible.

Pushing the chair back, I came to my feet hurriedly. "Good morning, Mrs. Maddigan," I blurted. "Come in."

She smiled at me, her full lips still pouting; she must have practiced that. "I *am* in, Jeb," she said.

I held the chair which ten minutes ago had contained her nephew, and sat down. She looked about the cubbyhole I call my office while I returned to my own chair and tried to look business-like.

"Private detectives don't *seem* to do any too well," she said, wrinkling up her nose distastefully.

"The bigger agencies make out," I told her. "The smaller ones are like just about any other small business; most of us can't stand the competition from the larger outfits." I didn't offer her a drink, although the bottle stood open there on the desk before us. I figured that she, too, was decent people who wouldn't be drinking at ten in the morning. I must have guessed right; she didn't even look at it after that first crack.

She crossed her legs interestingly, but with nonchalance. I was revising some of the opinions I'd had of her the night before—in spite of the hangover, which should have kept such ideas from my head.

She took a cigarette from her bag, put it in her mouth and raised her neatly plucked eyebrows at me. I already had my box of kitchen matches in my hand. I struck one on the side of the box, held the flame momentarily until the sulphur burned away, and then lit up for her.

She blew a heavy cloud of bluish smoke from her mouth, and nodded at the box of overgrown matches. "Cute little lighter you've got there."

I nodded and sat back in my chair again. "The only one I've ever found that would always work," I told her seriously. "What can I do for you, Mrs. Maddigan?"

She made with her pout again. "Sandra."

"All right. What can I do for you, Sandra?"

She tapped the ash from her cigarette onto the floor; not deliberately. It was just that it never occurred to her to reach out for the ashtray, three feet in front of her. But I still didn't like it. "Jeb," she said, letting just a hint of frown touch her forehead, "I want to hire you to investigate the death of Harry Shulman. Can you come over to the apartment this afternoon and discuss it?"

I must have stared at her stupidly at first, but finally I got out, "Why?"

She made with her moué again, but this time her eyes wouldn't meet mine. "Do I have to tell you why?" she asked.

I looked at her for another long moment. "No," I said. "No, you don't, but whatever the reason, the answer is *no.*"

She didn't get that. "You mean you won't take the job?"

I nodded definitely.

She plucked a shred of tobacco off her lip and frowned, more deeply this time. "Well, why?"

I got a shell brier out of the top drawer and drew the pound tin of Raleigh over toward me. I filled it carefully before answering her. I couldn't get the angle.

"Were you a particularly close friend of Harry Shulman's?" I began.

She shook her head at me. "I told you I wouldn't tell why I wanted his death investigated. But, Jeb, a job is a job, isn't it?

What reason could you possibly have for turning down this one? My money should be—" She broke off and narrowed her eyes at me. "You don't already have a client?"

I shook my head negatively. "Look," I told her, "I've already been through this once this morning, so I'll cut it short. In spite of the stories you've read, private detectives don't take homicide cases. Among other reasons, they're not allowed to mess around in business that is strictly that of the homicide detail. Our friend, Lieutenant Davis, would take a very dim view of my poaching on his preserves. Aside from that, Mr. Davis can and will find the cause for Shulman's death. It's doubtful if I could."

She pouted again. "I don't have much confidence in the police when it comes to an affair like this."

I put my elbows on the desk, touched fingertips to fingertips and tried to make my voice judicious. "You should have," I told her. "Certainly they're better equipped to work it out than is anyone else."

She finished her cigarette, dropped it on my floor and neatly crushed it out with the heel of her pump.

"Then there's no way in which I can persuade you to . . ."

I shook my head again. "No. You've just got the wrong idea of what a private investigator is and what he's capable of accomplishing, Sandra."

She stood up, looking at me in rising irritation. She snapped, "You look like quite a bit of a man, but you certainly don't act like one."

The door slammed behind her.

I said to myself, *Now I wonder what she wanted, really,* and went back to the bottle on the desk again. I was having quite a time trying to get around to those eyeopeners.

I was just finishing my first drink when I saw two shadows through the translucent glass. I whipped the bottle and glass off the desk top and into the bottom drawer and came to my feet.

"Oh, my aching back," I muttered.

"What was that?" James Maddigan asked, entering. Art Roget brought up the rear.

"Good morning," I told them, striving to keep bitterness from my voice. "Sit down. I know: You want me to investigate Shulman's death."

Maddigan's lips were tight, giving him his characteristic peevish expression. He looked about for a chair in which to lower his bulk before he answered. He settled himself pompously, then said, "Not exactly."

Roget found a chair too. That grin of his seemed to be gone with the snows of yesteryear. He looked worried now, like Jimmy Stewart that time he was a senator in Washington and discovered some of the boys were nothing but nasty old politicians.

"Well, you're at least different," I said.

Maddigan eyed me sharply now. "What was that?"

I hunched my right shoulder. "In the past hour I've had two persons up here wanting to hire me to show the police how to do their duty in connection with the Shulman death."

"Who were they?" He sounded eager, and his right hand went out to stroke his knee.

I shook my head. "Can't tell. Ethics, or something."

"Well, then, you accepted?"

I shook my head. "Nope. That's police business. I keep my nose out of it."

He relaxed and thought it over for a minute. Finally he said, "Art Roget and I think there is something wrong here."

"Ummm," I told him, taking up the pipe again and reaching for my matches. "Murder is always wrong."

"That's not what we mean," Maddigan said uncomfortably. "We don't think the police are going to find the killer, Mr. Knight."

I shook out the match I'd just struck, and put my pipe down unlit. "Listen," I said patiently. "This is the third time I've been through this. I'm going to boil it all the way down. The police department is better equipped to find murderers than are private detectives."

Roget cleared his throat. "When the murderer is a human," he muttered petulantly.

I turned my eyes to him and then back to Maddigan. "Oh, no," I complained.

Madigan ignored that. He shook a thick finger at me. "Knight," he said, "when we came up here the other day, none of us believed—really believed—the story we gave you. As we told Lieutenant Davis last night, our hiring your services was a humorous stunt for the convention."

He waved his right hand deprecatingly. "Oh, I'll admit some of us fen have had suspicions that aliens were already present here on earth; some of us have even made regular hobbies of investigating such possibilities. Harry Shulman in particular was quite convinced of the presence of aliens from space."

Art Roget frowned and started to add something, but Maddigan motioned him to silence and went on. "Frankly, I haven't been one of these. I appreciate fantasy and science fiction, but I don't become serious over the stories I read. However . . ."

"Wait a minute," I interrupted. "Without stringing this out too long, are you telling me that you two have come to the conclusion that young Shulman was bumped off by one of our little green friends?"

Maddigan frowned deeply and his jowls quivered protest. "That isn't exactly the way I would put it, Mr. Knight." He pounded his knee earnestly four or five times, searching for the way he *would* put it. "Let us say this: Shortly after being a party to hiring you to investigate the presence of aliens on earth, Harry Shulman was killed under circumstances which seem utterly impossible."

"All right," I sighed. "Where do I come in? What did you want?"

Maddigan leaned forward earnestly, resting a heavy hand on the desk edge. "We want you to continue the investigation, Mr. Knight."

I had felt it coming for several minutes, so I was able to take it without flinching. "No," I said emphatically.

He was surprised. "But why not?"

"Listen, I'm a private investigator, Maddigan. I don't mess in homicide cases."

He shook his heavy face impatiently, his jowls wobbling. "You don't understand. We are not hiring you to investigate Harry's murder—if it was murder. We want you to find out whether or not there are aliens from space here on earth." He shrugged beefy shoulders. "Of course, there might well be a certain degree of overlapping of the two cases . . ."

I growled, "A certain amount is good." But I was thinking it over in spite of myself. Twenty-five bucks a day looked awfully desirable.

Maddigan said, "Let me put it this way. Above your regular rates I shall let you have a bonus of five hundred dollars if you either prove, or disprove—which would be rather difficult, I admit—the presence of such aliens."

I rubbed my neck savagely. "Well," I growled finally, "I'll try it. I still think the two of you are missing some marbles on this; but as I keep saying, it's your money."

Maddigan was reaching for his wallet. He said, "Of course, as mentioned, there will be some overlapping of your work with the police investigation of Harry's demise. I assume that you have enough in the way of connections at headquarters so that you'll be able to check with them on anything you need?"

"Yeah," I said, watching him extract bills from a heavy wallet. "Yeah, I know a couple of the boys from army days. I can get anything I need from them."

He handed me seventy-five dollars. "Another thing," he asked. "Who were the two persons who wanted to hire you for the case this morning?"

I shook my head. "Sorry, the ethics still apply."

"But you're now in our employ."

"Sorry, gentlemen."

Maddigan pursed his full lips peevishly. "Very well," he said stiffly. He rose to his feet. "Of course, as before, you will make complete daily reports on your progress."

I eyed him suspiciously. "Listen," I said, "you sure this isn't going to wind up as a gag for your convention?"

CHAPTER SIX

Jّ AMES MADDIGAN said steadily, "You are being employed to investigate the possibility of alien life forms being here on earth, nothing else."

"All right," I said. "When—and if—Davis drags down the killer of Shulman, that'll at least be negative evidence. Right now you think the fact that the killing took place is possible evidence in favor of these, uh, aliens, being present?"

He pursed his lips. "Possible evidence. It would seem too much of a coincidence . . ."

I interrupted with, "Listen, there must have been twenty-five persons there last night. Do you actually believe one of them might be a Martian or a Venusian?"

Art Roget grinned wryly. "It sounds kind of crazy when you come right out with it like that, doesn't it?"

"Yes," I said.

Maddigan was frowning in irritation. "Of course it does, but that's beside the point."

"All right," I said. "Would it be possible for me to get a list of those present last night?"

Art Roget said, "I'm the recording secretary of the club. I have a list here." He was reaching into an inner coat pocket. "It has all the members and their addresses. Of course, they weren't all at Ross's last night. Here, I'll cross out those that weren't. Then, let's see, there were several non-members. You, and Mrs. Maddigan, and Ross's girl friend."

"Julie Sharp," I said.

He looked up. "Is that her name? I've never really met her."

I took the list of names from him and went down it. Twenty-four names altogether, including Julie and Sandra.

"One other thing," I told them. "You mentioned that Harry Shulman was pretty keen on this theory that there are aliens on earth. Now that he's gone, who on this list would you say knew most about that subject?"

Art Roget didn't have to think about it. "Les Zimmer," he said immediately. "Les is a regular fanatic on extra-terrestrials."

I checked Zimmer's name on my list and thought it over for a minute. "Anything else you can think of that might help?" I asked them.

They shook their heads in unconscious unison. I led them to the door and we went through the usual banalities of breaking company.

When they were gone I went back to the desk and sank into my chair. "My roof is probably leaking," I growled to myself. "Aliens from space, yet."

I looked down into the bottom drawer sadly. There was my bottle with only one drink out of it, and that dying in me fast. I regarded the fifth thoughtfully but finally gave it up. I went over to the washbowl and got myself a paper towel and wadded it up to improvise as a cork. It'd do well enough as long as the bottle was standing on end. I put the whiskey back into the drawer, closed it, and reached for the phone.

I dialed police headquarters, asked for the homicide bureau and then Herman Cain. I told him who I was, and we growled back and forth cheerfully for a minute before he asked me what I wanted.

"Some dope on the Harry Shulman case, Hermie," I told him, trying to keep a nonchalant tone in my voice.

He was still for a minute. "You know better than that, Jeb."

Not that he could see me, but I shook my head earnestly. "It isn't what you think, Herm. I've got a different case, but one that hinges on Shulman's. Listen, what I want to know is if Davis has lined up anybody for the rap so far."

He said hesitantly, "No. Not yet."

"Well, this is what I really need. Has he located a motive for the death?"

Hermie Cain hesitated longer this time. "Maybe I shouldn't tell you this, Jeb," there was puzzlement in his voice, "but that's the funniest thing about this deal. There *isn't* any motive. That kid didn't have an enemy in the world, no money, not even a girl. We can't dig up anybody who could profit by his being chilled; the only conceivable angle is that a crackpot killed him. You know all these characters are hot for this screwy science fiction stuff anyway. Mike Quinn—he's the sergeant working with Davis on this case—thinks one of them might have slipped his cogs."

"Wouldn't be surprised," I grunted.

"Well, anyway, short of that, there just isn't any reason why anybody'd want to kill Harry Shulman."

I thought that over.

Hermie Cain's voice came back. "You still there, Jeb?"

"Yeah," I said. "Yeah. Well, thanks, Herm. I'll be seeing you. We'll have to get together some night and bend a few elbows. Maybe we can ring Marty Rhuling in on it."

"Good enough, Jeb. And look, it better not get back to Davis that I've been . . ."

"All right," I muttered. "So long, Herm." I hung up.

I stared down at the phone nestled in its cradle. "No motive," I told myself. I got to my feet and went looking for my hat. "No motive except that he suspected there were aliens here on earth. Men from Mars. Straight out of an Orson Welles deal—or maybe Alley Oop."

I locked the door behind me, pocketed the key and walked down the steps to the lobby, not wanting to wait for Mike and his tired elevator. On the street, I stood there before the Kroll Building and ran my eyes over the list of names Art Roget had given me. Harry Shulman's was near the top; he'd been the club's treasurer. I let the thought trickle through my mind momentarily that that might have had something to do with it, but shrugged it away impatiently. There wouldn't be enough dough in the treasury of a club no bigger than Scylla to get anybody worked up about it.

I walked slowly to the corner of Marion and West Second and to the cab stand there, and climbed into the Checker at the head of the line. Shulman's house was within easy distance; I gave the driver the number and on the way tried to work over what I had to go on. I didn't get very far. I didn't have anything to work with. The whole situation was crazy.

Being hired to find aliens from space was crazy.

Harry Shulman's being killed was crazy—there was no motive.

His method of dying was crazy.

Three different parties wanting to hire me to investigate the matter was crazy. Everybody knew I was the lousiest detective in the city, if not in the nation.

By the time I'd got down through half a dozen more things about this case that were crazy, we'd reached the Shulman address and I was climbing out of the cab and paying the driver off.

320 West Seventh Street was the most average-looking house in the United States, if that makes sense to you. It was red brick and wood and probably about twenty-five years old. It wasn't going to get much older and be able to keep up decent pretenses; even a fairly recent coat of paint hadn't completely disguised the

fact that the lumber used in its construction could have been better grade. The foundation hadn't exactly been tops either; there were cracks between some of the bricks. There was a futile attempt at a lawn, a sad-looking lilac bush to one side. While I stood there, a Monarch butterfly dragged wearily through the air and landed on a tired flower. It moved its wings up and down a few times, then took off again as though in disgust.

I walked up the cracked concrete walk to the steps of the little house and knocked on the side of the screen door. The house door was open, homage to the day's rapidly increasing temperature, but the screen was latched. I knocked again, louder.

I could see her, then, coming down the hallway from the kitchen at the rear of the house. Her very appearance screamed *mother*. She was frail, faded, gray; stamped with the perpetual tiredness of the housewife serving a life term and who has never had quite enough security.

I took off my hat and said, "Mrs. Shulman?"

She wiped her hands on her apron and nodded. "Yes, I'm Mrs. Shulman."

I said, "I'd like to speak to you if I may."

Weariness came over her face and she sighed. "You're from another of the newspapers?"

I shook my head. "No, Mrs. Shulman, I'm not. I'm a detective."

She frowned. "But I've told Lieutenant Davis all I know already. He said I wouldn't be bothered again unless it was very important. I—I—" She was on the verge of breaking down.

"I have a particular interest in the case," I said hurriedly. "You see, I knew Harry." I left it there for a minute; then, "I *would* like to talk to you."

She was tired, bone-tired. She said softly and slowly, "What difference does it make now? Harold is gone. It wouldn't bring him back even though you caught this person who didn't want Harold to live any more."

I said gently, "There's one fault in your reasoning, Mrs. Shulman. I agree with you in principle: revenge is a worthless thing; but you see, there may be other Harrys—Harolds—and other parents. If your son's murderer is allowed to go on he'll find new victims. To protect itself, society must root out those persons capable of killing."

She reached out a worn hand and flicked the latch on the door. "Come in, please," she said softly. She turned and led the way to the living room. I followed her, hat in hand.

Undoubtedly, the Shulman family had been of the old school. The parlor was a show room; they had done their living in a large kitchen.

She settled herself in an uncomfortable-looking easy chair, and folded her hands on her lap. I sat on the rust-colored mohair sofa, long from the mail-order house but showing little wear.

"I'm sure that there isn't anything I can add to what I told the other policemen," she said, resignation in her voice.

I didn't answer that. I said, "Mrs. Shulman, the greatest difficulty seems to be finding a reason why anyone should want to kill Harry. You've probably heard of the old police adage: Find the motive. Usually, if you find out why a person was killed, you can fairly easily find out by whom he was killed."

She nodded wearily, "Yes, I know. Lieutenant Davis told me that they couldn't discover a purpose for Harold's—Harold's—"

I went on hurriedly. "Then you can think of no reason why anyone should want him dead?"

She shook her head. "No, Harold had no enemies at all. Mr.—"

"Knight," I told her.

"Mr. Knight, he was just a boy. Why, he hardly had any interests at all, aside from his reading and the science fiction club, and his job."

"Where did he work?"

"Why, I've already told all this. Harold was fountain manager of the Rexall drug store on Stark and Tenth."

I took the list that Art Roget had given me and handed it to her. "Mrs. Shulman, do you recognize any of these names as anyone that Harry was particularly close to, or anyone he had business connections with—or even romantic ones?"

She looked at the names. "Why, yes, I recognize some of these. Harold was treasurer of the Scylla Club, you know." There was a faint trace of pride in that. "Let me see; here is Lester Zimmer. Lester used to come to dinner sometimes. And here is Ross Maddigan; Harold talked about him from time to time. And Arthur Roget, he's been here for dinner, too. They used to put out a mimeographed little magazine together about two years ago, Lester and Arthur and Harold."

"Off-Trail Fantasy?" I suggested.

"Oh, gracious, no. No, this was two magazines ago. Harold puts—did put—out his new magazine all by himself. He has a place of his own down in the cellar for his magazines and his mimeograph machine and things."

She looked again at the list. "I'm afraid that those are the only names I recogniize, Mr. Knight."

"You don't see any that Harry might have been connected with outside of his Scylla Club membership? Someone . . ."

Mrs. Shulman was shaking her head again. "No, I don't believe so."

"About these names you have mentioned—Zimmer, Roget and Ross Maddigan—did Harry have any connection with them aside from their mutual interest in science fiction?"

"I don't think so, Mr. Knight."

"You don't believe that it might be possible that Harry found out something—something very important —about one of them?"

"I can't imagine such a thing. He hasn't given any such indication around the house, and usually Harold told me just about everything." She'd been holding up well thus far, but now I could see her defenses crumbling. I came quickly to my feet.

"All right, Mrs. Shulman. Thank you very much. I'll be going now. No, don't bother; I can find my way out. Thank you again."

She had a handkerchief to her eyes as I left the room and made my way to the screen door. I felt like a heel. Who was I to break in on her sorrow?

It was harder to find a cab this time. I told myself that I should have had the other one wait.

Montgomery Boulevard was about three blocks south. I walked over to it, on the way trying to get something out of what Mrs. Shulman had told me. There wasn't anything, at least not that I could put my finger on.

I reached the boulevard and stood waiting for a cab or a bus. At last I hailed a cab and got in.

The driver said, "Where to?" looking over his shoulder at me.

I reached absently for my list of names. I read off Les Zimmer's number, 632 Lafayette Avenue, and settled back.

"What's the matter, buddy," the cabby said sarcastically, "you tired?" I didn't get it.

He swung the cab around the corner, drove up one block and half a block over and pulled up to the curb. I looked at my list again, and up at the street number. Les Zimmer lived about a block and a half away from Harry Shulman's home.

The driver looked back at me. "Thirty-five cents," he said, sneering.

To hell with trying to explain. I counted out exactly thirty-five cents and handed it to him. If he expected a tip, he could whistle for it.

He snorted, shot into low gear and was off.

I looked up at the Zimmer home. Possibly ten years newer, otherwise it was almost a duplicate of the Shulman house. There seemed to be a little more time and a little more money involved, too; not much, but some. A neater lawn, a fairly nice hedge fence.

I went up the walk, rang the bell, and waited.

He came finally, his hands dirty with printer's ink, a printer's apron around him to protect his clothes, and an impatient expression on his face. Another kid, perhaps twenty or so; Shulman's age. His nose was too big and his eyes prominent and too sincere; his ears stuck out from the side of his head like Bing Crosby's. I remembered having seen him at Ross Maddigan's party. He was one of those who had fumed against the use of pen-names.

He opened the door and said, "I'm sorry, but I'm busy and the lady of the house . . ."

Evidently he didn't recognize me. "I'm not selling anything," I told him. "My name's Job Knight; I wanted to talk to you. You're Les Zimmer, aren't you?"

He placed me now. "My name is Lester Zimmer, yes. You're the private detective, aren't you?" he said. His voice was a bit on the high side, something like Shulman's. The two had more in common than science fiction; they could have been brothers.

"That's right," I told him.

For a minute, I thought he was going to close the door in my face, but then, suddenly, he opened it.

"Come on in," he said. "We'll have to go down to the basement. I've got ink on the platen of my press and I can't let it dry." He led the way down a hall to a cellar door and then down a dozen steps to his sanctum. Evidently he'd taken the basement over lock stock and barrel for his hobby. The walls were lined with bookshelves he'd improvised from unfinished lumber; there were rows and rows of them, filled with pulp magazines.

He had one manufactured bookcase, glass-enclosed, and obviously picked up at a second hand furniture shop. It was well laden with hard cover volumes, most of them on the thick and battered side.

There were a dozen or so illustrations, obviously originals of art work that had appeared in the science fiction magazines—girls in scanty spacesuits, fantastic monsters being finished off with ray guns, time travelers finding themselves in the Roman arena. In one corner he had a small printing press, probably a six-by-nine, operated by a foot pedal arrangement. Near it was a rickety, ex-kitchen table with a flat piece of marble on it; his composing stone. Next to the table he had a home-made rack to hold half a dozen type cases which contained his scanty supply of type fonts.

The press platen was moist with ink and there was a form in place. He'd been running something off when I interrupted him. I look around interestedly while he went back to his press and started pumping it again. He'd pick up a dodger-size sheet of newsprint with his right hand, insert it in the press; then, while his left hand was extracting the finished product and putting it on a pile to his left, his right hand would insert another. All this time, his foot pumped up and down rapidly. He was getting as much speed as if he'd had an electric motor.

"You'll have to pardon me," he said, not very apologetically; "I'm running off some programs for the AnnCon." He didn't look up from his work to say it. "What can I do for you?"

I stood next to him and watched. His hands worked beautifully, in and out, in and out; you'd think he would have crushed them between the bed and the heavy form of type, but he had his coordination down pat. I'd hate to try it with a bun on.

I said, "Maddigan and Roget tell me you're quite an authority on the possibility of alien life forms being on earth."

He snorted disgustedly, and repeated, "What can I do for you, Mr. Knight?" I got the antagonism in his voice now, but I didn't understand it.

I took a deep breath and said, "I'm investigating the possibility?"

He stopped the press momentarily and looked over at me, his eyes earnest but unbelieving. He said, "I thought that was supposed to be a joke."

I said ruefully, "It was, two days ago. Roget and Maddigan seem to have changed their minds now."

He was too sincere to attempt to achieve sarcasm, but he expressed the nearest thing to it. "Isn't it rather silly for a grown man to be investigating the presence of aliens from space?"

I shrugged and got off a self-deprecating grin. "I'm a working man, Zimmer. I sell my time in return for money. If Maddigan and

Roget want to buy my time and use it for hunting out men from Mars . . ."

He looked at me, contempt growing in his expression. "You mean you'll take money for *anything*—"

"Not quite," I cut in, irritated.

"I'm afraid I can't help you, Mr. Knight," he said flatly. He turned back to his press and began pumping again. He reached with his right hand for a piece of the newsprint.

"Look," I told him, holding down my temper. "Art Roget says you're tops in this hobby of collecting dope on aliens from space. I thought you could give me a line on . . . "

"Sorry," he told me. "Can you find your way out?"

I looked at him in exasperation.

He said, still without looking up from his work, "It's one thing, making a hobby of finding evidence to indicate that space travel has already been achieved by intelligent life forms elsewhere in the universe; but when a disgusting murder has been committed, I can't see that such methods of confusing the issue will help any-one involved, except possibly the murderer. Can you find your way out, Mr. Knight?"

It was a pretty-effective brush-off, considering his youth.

CHAPTER SEVEN

IT LOOKED LIKE every other small apartment hotel in the world, complete to the no vacancy sign outside and a pimply, adolescent-looking clerk at the desk. I estimated that a small apartment at the Wentworth would run about seventy-five a month. No more than that, or the tenant was being robbed.

The clerk said, "Miss Sharp isn't in." He hadn't rung, and I looked at him quizzically.

He said, "She doesn't return until nearly six; she's at work. Miss Sharp has been with us for some time; she never gets home week days until nearly six."

I hadn't asked him for all that, but it was all right. I said, "Where does she work?"

He looked me over again, more carefully this time, taking in a suit that could soon use a pressing, and shoes that were beginning to show that they had seen endless shines and weren't taking them so well any more.

"I couldn't say," he said.

"Couldn't or wouldn't?"

"We don't give out information about our guests." His voice was stiff.

I carry a badge pinned in my wallet. I flashed it quickly, returned the wallet to my pocket and said, "I'm a detective, son. Where does Miss Sharp work?"

He looked at me levelly, "Let's have another look at that buzzer."

I grinned at him. "Okay," I said, "I'm a private eye; you don't have to tell me anything if you don't . . ."

"I don't, and won't," he said, satisfaction oozing from him.

There was a phone on the side of the desk. I checked quickly with my list, then picked it up and dialed. I said, "Ross Maddigan? This is Jeb Knight. Listen, in a way I've changed my mind about this case . . . Yeah. I'll see you later about it, probably tomorrow. But right now, could you tell me where Julie Sharp works? . . . No, of course not, but there were twenty-odd people there, and she was one of them . . . Of course, everybody . . . All right, see you later, thanks, Ross."

I hung up and turned back to the clerk. "You read too much Raymond Chandler," I said complacently.

"That will be a nickel for the call," he told me, cold-panned.

I grinned at him and flipped him his nickel. "You'll probably see more of me from now on, chum."

"I can't wait, shamus," he said between his teeth.

I started for the door. "What'd I tell you?" I said over my shoulder. "Too much reading about Philip Marlowe. Nobody ever calls anybody *shamus* outside of detective novels."

~ ~ ~ ~ ~

The textile firm for which Julie Sharp was working was located in the Wyandotte Building which is just about as far north of City Center as the Kroll Building, which houses *Lee and Knight, Private Investigations,* is to the south. That's the only similarity between the two buildings that I can think of. An elevator that zipped rather than rumbled, piloted by a uniformed little redhead who should have been in a chorus line, shot me up to the eighth floor in a matter of seconds. The elevator door opened out facing the heavy glass doors of Brandenburg and Sons.

I entered and asked the neat number at the PBX where I could find Julie Sharp. She directed me down a short corridor and to a door which stated, simply, *Joseph Brandenburg.* Beyond it was a small anteroom containing a neat little desk, two or three heavy, dark red leather reception room chairs, and the woman I couldn't get out of my mind.

When I entered, she looked up from her typewriter, frowning slightly at first. Then her generous mouth broke into a smile of recognition and her eyebrows twitched mischievously.

"Hi, shamus," she greeted me.

"Oh, *no,*" I grinned back at her, "I just got finished explaining that nobody ever really calls a private detective a shamus."

"Heavens, I'm disillusioned," she said, then shot a quick glance down at her watch. "I suppose this has something to do with last night. I hate to be rude, uh—" She was deciding what to call me.

"Jeb," I said.

"—but I'll only be able to give you five minutes. Mr. Brandenburg . . ."

"All right," I told her. "Shouldn't be bothering you during working hours anyway; perhaps I could see you later."

Her eyebrow went up. "This *is* business, I suppose."

I nodded very seriously.

She took her hands away from the typewriter, checked something on the paper she'd been working at with her pencil, then turned back to me. "Very well," she said, "sit down and tell me what I can do."

I sank into one of the leather chairs and said slowly, "I thought that being an outsider at that party might have given you a slightly different viewpoint. That you might have seen something that another would have let go by."

She frowned prettily and pursed her lips, but she didn't say anything.

"How well did you know Harry Shulman?" I asked her.

She twitched one shoulder—once again, prettily. "I knew him just slightly, through Ross. He seemed to be a nice enough kid."

"When did you see him last?"

She only had to think a few seconds about that. "When he came into the kitchen and hauled you off, I believe."

"Ummm," I said. "He wanted to show me the latest issue of his fanzine. In fact, he was a mite upset about my not reading it on the spot, gave me a copy to take along." I broke off, then asked, "Can you think of any reason why anyone would want to murder him?"

She put her hand to her mouth thoughtfully, the nail of her little finger touching her teeth, finally shook her head. "It's fantastic." Her eyes were candid and convincing.

I got a sudden inspiration. "Listen, could it have been a mistake? Is it possible that someone might have been after, oh, say, Ross, or Jim Maddigan, or Roget, or one of the others, and killed Harry accidentally?"

She stared at me, her violet-tinged eyes slightly wider than ordinarily. "Well—I don't know. The only ones there I knew at all were Ross, his uncle, and . . ." she wrinkled her nose distastefully. ". . . Sandra. Oh, I know several of them to speak to, but not well enough to be familiar with their private affairs."

I followed the thread of idea I'd got. "Well, how about Ross? It was his house; possibly someone was after him."

She shook her head emphatically. "Not Ross. I've never met anyone more personally popular than Ross Maddigan; it's his greatest fault as far as I'm concerned. Everybody loves Ross.

Heavens, I get tired of it." She smiled again, as though to take some of the barb off that.

"But how about his finances—something along that line?"

She laughed lightly. "Ross doesn't know or care anything about finances. His uncle runs the business and turns over to him more than he could possibly use. You see, James Maddigan and Ross's father were business partners. After Ross's father died, it was agreed that Ross wasn't suited to enter Maddigan and Maddigan. An arrangement was made so that he continued to receive dividends, but he has practically no interest in the business otherwise. Ross is trying to break into writing, you know."

"How about Sandra? You said you knew her."

The expression of distaste again; evidently there was little love lost between the girls. "Do you mean, would it be possible that she was trying to kill Ross, or her husband, and made the mistake of killing Harry Shulman instead?"

That was too bald. "Not necessarily," I said. "Perhaps it could have been the other way around. Possibly someone was trying to kill Sandra and got Harry by mistake."

Julie shot another quick glance at her watch, but evidently we still had a few minutes. "This is rather digging into family affairs," she said, "but I don't imagine it will harm anything to tell you that James Maddigan is rather jealous of Sandra." She took her lower lip in her small teeth momentarily, as thought wondering whether to go on. "With *some* reason. However, I can't picture any of the three of them wishing to kill one of the others." She shook her head deprecatingly. "Heavens, that's really inconceivable."

I was drawing another blank. I said, "And you don't know any of the others well enough to comment at all?"

Julie moved her head slowly. "Afraid not." She looked at her watch again. "I really should be getting back to work."

I came to my feet. "About seeing you later—in case I have some other things to ask?"

"Are you certain it's strictly business?"

"Not too certain—but *some* business."

Her smile flashed again. "If you'd said yes, I would have said no. But not tonight, Jeb; I have a date tonight."

"With Ross?"

Her eyebrows went up.

I said hurriedly, "I was figuring on seeing him later. If he's going to be out . . ."

She nodded. "With Ross." She added, "We're engaged, you know." Then, again irrelevantly, "Are you going to attend the Convention? It starts day after tomorrow."

"Convention? Oh, you mean the AnnCon—isn't that what they call it?"

I scowled. "I don't know."

"Do you think there'll be any extra-terrestrials?"

She played it straight. "Perhaps."

I let my right shoulder rise and drop sadly. "I guess I'll have to go and find out for myself."

~ ~ ~ ~ ~

I'd eaten too late in the afternoon to be interested in supper at my usual time. Instead, I walked down to City Center, dropped into the Walgreen Drug Store on the corner of Stark and Montgomery and got myself two bottles of ginger ale and three lemons. Then I walked the remaining three blocks to the Kroll Building.

The elevator grumbled me up to my floor and I shifted my package to my left arm, got out my keys and opened up. There wasn't any mail, not even bills or ads, this time. I put my stuff on the desk, took off my coat and hat and hung them up, then reached into the closet for the old battered portable I kept in there.

I sat in on the desk top and took off the cover. My glass and bottles were still in the big lower drawer; I reached down and brought them forth. The paper towel I'd stuck in the bottle mouth in lieu of the cork I'd pushed down into the bottle was moist; one end of it had evidently got into the whiskey and capillary action had soaked up some of the liquid. I swore mildly and threw my improvised stopper into the waste basket.

I poured a slug of the whiskey into the glass and got my pocket knife out to cut a lemon in half. I didn't have a squeezer, so I had to do the best I could with my hands. I squeezed half a lemon into the glass, then filled the tumbler with ginger ale. I should have got some ice at the drug store while I was at it. The first couple of drinks would be cool, but from there on . . .

I got some of our nicely printed letterheads and some carbons out of another drawer and sighed as I cranked them into the portable. This was where my real work began. I started pounding away with two fingers.

REPORT ON INVESTIGATION INTO POSSIBILITIES OF
ALIEN LIFE FORMS FROM SPACE BEING
PRESENT ON EARTH

From: Lee and Knight, Private Investigations

To: James L. Maddigan and Arthur Roget

Gentlemen: I began the day's efforts by getting in touch with sources on the police force in an attempt to ascertain whether or not there was *human* motive for the death of Harry Shulman. Thus far, the police have evidently found no such motivation, according to my well informed contact.

In an attempt to check further upon this aspect of the case, I then proceeded to the Shulman home. "Questioning of Mrs. Shulman only bore out the findings of the police . . ."

~ ~ ~ ~ ~

I kept at it for almost an hour because that sort of thing comes hard to me. I'd rather make an oral report any day in the week.

As I worked, I filled my glass from time to time. I'd been right; I should have got ice. The first two or three drinks weren't bad, but when the ginger ale got warm in the bottle they started to pall on me.

When I was finished, I folded the report in an envelope, fished in my wallet for a book of three cent stamps, then sealed and stamped it.

I yawned and looked out the window. It was beginning to get dark outside, and the evening was beginning to cool off. I improvised another stopper for my whiskey and got up to get my coat and hat. The hangover I'd started the day with was gone, but I still felt like a character out of Erich Maria Remarque— you know, *The Road Back,* the lost generation. I didn't know where the hell I was, where I was going, or why I wanted to get there.

You don't know what I'm talking about? Okay, let's hope you never learn.

I slapped the battered felt on the back of my head, stuck my hands in my pockets and headed for Sam's Bar down the street.

CHAPTER EIGHT

YESTERDAY, the morning after the night before had been bad enough. This was worse. I should have known better than to hang one on right on top of another. I got to the office at about ten o'clock, one hour later than standard, feeling that I was lucky to have made it at all.

Sergeant Mike Quinn, Lieutenant Davis' companion the night of the Shulman killing, was leaning at the side of my door, chewing complacently on an unlit cigar. When he saw me, he grinned, took the cigar from his mouth and said with mock pleasantness, "The lieutenant wants to see you, Buster."

"Davis?"

"That's right, Buster. Come along."

My mind was chugging along on two cylinders. I scowled at him and said, "What for?"

His grin broadened. "That's a secret, Buster; but I'll bet you can guess." He'd evidently been seeing too many crime movies; he sounded more like a movie cop than Dick Powell.

"All right," I said wearily; "let me check to see if I've got any mail."

"Okay," he agreed, "but you better hurry it up. You always keep these hours? I don't know why I don't turn private."

"Sure," I grunted, getting my key out and inserting it in the Yale lock. He evidently expected me to get off some snappy rejoinder, but I wasn't up to being very snappy. "I get to work at about ten. At noon I take three hours off for lunch. Then I knock off for the day at four."

He yawned disinterestedly and mumbled something appropriate. The door swung open and we entered. I stooped to pick up the two unimpressive-looking envelopes that had been thrust under the door, and at the same time the phone rang.

I went over and picked up the receiver from its cradle and said, "Jeb Knight speaking."

It was James Maddigan. He said peevishly, "I haven't as yet received your daily report for yesterday, Knight."

I was peevish myself. I said, "I put it in the mail last night. If you haven't got it this morning it'll probably be in the afternoon delivery; if it isn't, blame it on Uncle Sam."

He muttered something I didn't make out, then said, "Knight, Roget and I are thinking of discontinuing this investigation. We've been discussing it with some of the other Scylla Club members, and the more we think about it the more ridiculous it sounds."

"That's what I told you in the first place," I said impatiently. "You want me to knock off, then?"

He hummed and hawed a bit. "Well, let us say this, Knight. Continue on the investigation until the money we advanced you is expended. You didn't discover anything of moment yesterday, did you?"

"I told him I hadn't.

"Very well, then; I'll expect to receive your reports for, let me see, two more days, wouldn't it be?"

"That's right," I said.

He said goodbye absently, and hung up.

"Who was that?" Mike Quinn asked.

I shot an irritated glance at him and tried to make like Nick Charles. "My Grandmother. She wants to know if I can pick her up a date for tonight."

"Okay, Buster. Let's get going. The longer you keep Davis waiting, the less happy he's going to be about you, and he's none too happy now, Buster."

I followed him out into the hall again and began to relock the door. Both of the letters had been bills.

Just as the tumbler clicked, the phone began to ring.

Quinn muttered, "What is this; the telephone exchange?"

"Hold it a minute," I told him. I reopened the door and crossed to the desk and took up the receiver again.

"Jeb Knight," I said.

A voice squeaked, "This is Lester Zimmer. Listen, Mr. Knight, I have to see you right away."

"Ummmm," I said. "So does Lieutenant Davis of the homicide detail."

"You mean you can't come?" Zimmer shrilled.

"Not for a while. What's it all about?"

"Well, you know that information you wanted yesterday?" He didn't wait for an affirmation, but blurted on, "I've got some soul-shaking information for you. Can't you postpone your other appointment?"

Soul-shaking, yet; the boy was absolutely lyrical. I looked over at Mike Quinn. "I doubt it," I told the phone. "I'll have to see you later."

There were indications of near-hysteria in his voice. "I'll lock all the doors until you come," he shrilled. "You don't think this phone has been tapped, do you?"

"I doubt it," I said. "I'll be over as soon as I can make it." I dropped the phone back onto its cradle and stared down at it for a minute.

Quinn said, "I suppose that was your other grandmother."

I shook my head absently, still wondering what Zimmer could be so worked up about. "My grandfather. He wants a blonde. It's disgusting the way those two cheat on each other."

"Let's go," he grunted. "I got a sneaking suspicion you're going to lose some of that wit of yours this morning, Buster."

Mike Quinn had a police car parked in front of the Kroll Building. Somehow or other, I'd missed noticing it on the way up. A uniformed patrolman, his face expressionless, but somehow radiating boredom, was sitting in the driver's seat.

"Now you probably think this is real style, Buster," Mike Quinn told me, opening the rear door for me with undue ceremony. "I'll bet you usually get drug in in the paddy wagon."

I didn't answer him. We got in the back and the driver clashed into gear and took off without turning around. He zipped east on Marion Avenue to East First, where he turned left up to Lafayette. The decrepit Justice Building is on the corner of Lafayette and East First; he zoomed up the wide driveway, lined on both sides with official cars, and to the rear where he ground to a halt before the back entrance.

Quinn and I piled out, and the driver, still without looking around, clashed back into gear again and was off.

I said bitterly, "Another few lessons and he should be able to get a license." My hangover wasn't up to that kind of driving.

Quinn growled something that ended in "Buster" and led the way up the stone steps to the aged halls of the Justice Building. We turned left at the first stairway and climbed the wooden steps to the second floor. Halfway down the musty corridor and opposite a water-cooler, once painted white, was a door lettered, *Lieutenant Philip Davis,* and, under that, *Homicide Detail.*

Quinn gave a flip of a knock and opened the door before getting a response. We went in. It was a small room with splotched brown walls; drab, friendless, and the one window translucent with gray dirt.

Lieutenant Davis was sitting behind a battered desk strewn with a multitude of papers; the surface remaining indicated long years of cigarette burns and endless scratching from the heels of over-sized shoes. His face was even more pale in the light of day; he reminded you of a white grub worm under the log you kick over during a hike in the woods. His colorless eyes were unblinking. He said sarcastically, "Our busy little beaver is here at last."

"Good morning," I told him. "To what do I owe the pleasure of this pinch?"

"Sit down," he said. "It isn't a pinch—yet. And don't crack wise. That's all I need; a wise guy."

I found myself a chair and lowered myself into it, reaching in my coat for my pipe. I brought it out and a tin of Raleigh from the opposite pocket.

Davis said almost apologetically, "I can't stand smoke—asthma."

I put the pipe back into my pocket, and looked at him.

He took up a sheet of paper from his desk. "Yesterday morning at nine thirty-two Ross Maddigan went into your office. Ten minutes after he left, Sandra Maddigan went in, barely missing him in the elevator. Quarter of an hour after she left, James Maddigan and Arthur Roget went in and stayed for another thirty minutes or so. After they left you went to the Shulman house and questioned Mrs. Shulman, giving her the impression you were a police officer." His scanty brows went up and he shot me a quick glance from expressionless eyes. "That, by the way—impersonating an officer—is actionable, Knight." His eyes went back to his paper and he went on. "Leaving the Shulman home, you went to that of Lester Zimmer, remaining inside for approximately ten minutes. Afterward, you went to the apartment house in which Miss Julie Sharp lives and again attempted to impersonate an officer in order to extract information from the desk clerk. After that, you went to Miss Sharp's place of employment and spent fifteen or twenty minutes talking to her."

He tossed the paper to his desk and directed his gray eyes to me.

I looked back, trying to indicate that I was bewildered by all this.

He didn't add anything, so I tried to work some indignation into my tone, saying, "Listen, I deny impersonating an officer, Davis.

If either Mrs. Shulman or that desk clerk thought I was a cop, it wasn't my fault."

Davis growled, without taking his eyes from me, "What did Ross Maddigan want, eh?"

"He wanted to hire me to investigate the murder of Harry Shulman."

"Oh, brother," Mike Quinn muttered under his breath. Davis shot him an irritated glance.

"What did Sandra Maddigan want, Knight?"

"Same thing." I paused a moment, then added, "I turned them both down, of course, Lieutenant."

His eyes widened infinitesimally. "You did, eh? I was beginning to suspect you didn't have that much sense." He took a small bottle from a vest pocket and absently shook a pill into the palm of his hand. There was a cheap water carafe on the desk and a semiclean glass. He poured himself some water and washed his pill down before he said, "James Maddigan and his sidekick wanted the same thing, eh?"

I shook my head. "No, the older Maddigan and Art Roget wanted me to take a different case."

Davis bent forward toward me, leaning a scrawny elbow on the donk and resting his chin in a cupped hand. "What? What did they want you to do, eh?"

"Theoretically, I don't have to tell you."

Mike Quinn chuckled.

"That's right," Davis said softly, "theoretically you don't." His eyes were empty—emotionless and expressionless.

"It doesn't make any difference," I said hurriedly. "They wanted me to investigate the possible existence of alien life forms on earth."

Mike Quinn started laughing. "Here we go again," he said.

"Shut up, Mike," Davis growled. Then back at me, "I suppose you took that one, eh?"

I nodded. "That's right. I tried to talk them out of it, but if that's what they want, I'm in the business."

He rested his eyes on me unblinkingly for at least thirty seconds. Finally he said slowly, two faint spots of red burning in his hollow cheeks, "Listen, wise guy, if you think you're pulling my leg and getting away with it—they said the other night that that was just a gag for their convention."

I shrugged hugely. "They've evidently changed their minds now. Give them a ring if you don't believe me."

He snorted, and considered that for a while. Finally he looked up at me again. "Get out of here," he rasped.

~ ~ ~ ~ ~

So they had a tail on me. It wasn't bad enough that I had to take on jobs like searching out invaders from Jupiter, or wherever they were supposedly from, I had to have the homicide squad keeping track of my every move while I did it.

Mike Quinn hadn't offered to take me back to my office, so I retraced on foot the route our jitterbug driver had taken us over fifteen minutes earlier. I walked down East First to Marion, crossed the street and turned right. I made no effort to check on whether or not I had a tail.

On the way, I picked up an afternoon paper from a newsboy, and gave it a quick once-over as I walked. There wasn't anything new on the Shulman case. For some reason or other, it hadn't hit the headlines the way an off-trail murder usually will. Evidently there was too much public interest in the rapidly warming cold war.

I went to the Marion Street entrance, the main one, of the Kroll Building, as though heading for my office. But instead, I continued on back through the building to the small delivery door opening on the alley. I went down the alley to West First and turned right.

Half a block down I hailed a cab, piled in, and told the cabby to drive through traffic for a few minutes. I checked over my shoulder from time to time, but couldn't spot anything. I gave him Zimmer's address.

I kept my mind blank on the way over. On the phone, Les Zimmer had sounded as though he'd just got the word on where the Martians had landed and where they'd hid the spaceship. But there wasn't anything I could do about it until I talked to him. Something had changed his mind since yesterday; what it was I couldn't imagine and there was no use worrying about it.

I paid the driver off at the door and made my way up the walk and up the three wooden steps. The door was closed, in spite of the heat of the day. I rang the bell and waited.

Les Zimmer held aside the lace curtain and peered out fearfully. I looked over my shoulder just to be sure. There wasn't anything there.

He opened up a slit, just enough for my one hundred and eighty pounds of bulk, and I slipped in.

"What's the idea?" I asked. "Process server, or something?"

He didn't appreciate the try. His nose was still too big and his eyes too sincere, and his ears still stuck out from the side of his head like Bing Crosby's. But this time, on top of it all, he was scared spitless.

"I'm glad you finally got here," he said shrilly. His voice had been somewhat high the day before; now it was womanlike. It brought home to me how alike he and Harry Shulman were—or rather had been.

I pushed my hat to the back of my head and waited for him to go on.

He said, "Follow me, Mr. Knight," and turned and headed up the stairs to the second floor of the house. So it was Mr. Knight now. Evidently my standing had risen since our last tête-à-tête.

We went down the hallway half a dozen steps and he opened a door. I followed him inside. "This is my room," he said. "I slept here last night." His mouth twitched.

I started to say something like, "Congratulations," but broke it off halfway through. I pointed with my finger and said instead, "What the devil is that?"

The room was a small one with one window. His bed, a hard-looking, three quarter affair, sat opposite the window and about a foot from the wall. Under the window was a desk with an old Number 5 Underwood on it. There were two chairs, a five drawer bureau, a faded carpet on the floor. The walls were comparatively barren—a Varga calendar, a high school pennant, one magazine illustration original of the type he had in his den in the cellar.

My finger was pointing to a large, still slightly smoldering spot on the wall behind the bed. It was about three and a half or four feet in diameter and made a rough circle. The wall was a mess, he'd evidently thrown water on it to put out the fire.

"What happened?" I repeated.

He was actually trembling. "I'm not sure I know," he shrilled.

I turned and gave him a quick searching glance, then went over to the wall and scrutinized the spot carefully. "It looks like somebody went to work on your wall with a blow torch. When did it happen?"

"Last night."

I looked at him, curiously this time. "Well, where were you?"

"In bed, sleeping."

I didn't get it. It was clear to him, evidently, but I didn't get it at all. "What happened?" I asked him again.

His tongue darted out and licked his dry lips. "I went to bed a little early. When I woke up this morning, it was there, still smoking. It just missed me."

I still didn't get it. I looked back at the wall again. "What just missed you?"

"The heat ray. Don't you see?" he said shrilly. "They fired a heat ray at me."

CHAPTER NINE

I LET MY EYES go from Les Zimmer back to the wall and then to Zimmer again. "Never heard of it," I said. "Try to straighten up, man. What's a heat ray?"

He laughed, a high-pitched laugh. I grabbed him by the shoulder and shook him. "All right, snap out of it," I rapped. "You're acting like some dizzy blister. Now tell me what happened; give me more details."

He took a deep breath and then shook his head sharply. "Just a minute," he said. "I'll be all right. I'm sorry."

The apology was fine, but I preferred some sense. He crossed over to his desk and sat down at the low-back chair there. He took another deep breath or two and then looked up at me; his eyes were still as earnest as ever, but there was something wild in them, too.

"After you were here yesterday, I got to thinking about Arthur and James Maddigan hiring you. In fact, I became rather upset about it. Fandom is a serious matter to a good many of us, and we don't like to see it run into the ground. Time and again, the newspapers will ridicule us or outsiders will sneer, 'Buck Rogers stuff.' Actually, as Tony Boucher, one of the staff editors, put it once, Buck Rogers has about the same relationship to science fiction as Dick Tracy has to the detective novel."

"All right, aren't you drifting away from the point?" I asked him impatiently. "I know some of you fans bleed about this stuff."

He took another deep breath. "Well, I thought that some of the members of Scylla—and Scylla is probably the most advanced club in the country—hiring a private detective to look for aliens would just give outsiders another opportunity to ridicule the science fiction field. I decided to go to Maddigan and protest. So early that evening I took my car and drove over to the Maddigan home. Arthur Roget was already there and they'd already been arguing. Not that they were making any sense; first one would argue on one side, and then he'd switch over to the other."

"What were they arguing about?"

"About whether or not it was sensible to hire you. Well, I got into it and we had it hot and heavy for a while. Maddigan is only a half-baked fan anyway, as far as I can see. Arthur is more of a student, although even Arthur leans more to fantasy." Les Zimmer sneered. "He thinks the *Magazine of Fantasy and Science Fiction* is superior to *Astounding.*"

"Listen," I signed, "let's get to the point."

"Well, we argued a while and finally they decided I was right and that they'd call you off."

"My pal," I muttered.

"It's not that I have anything against you, Mr. Knight," Zimmer said earnestly, his big ears going slightly red.

I didn't say anything, so he went on. "Afterwards, I drove home, planning on doing some more work on the programs for the Anniversary Convention. I'm spending my vacation, you know, working for the AnnCon." He added irrelevantly, "Mother and Father have gone to the Adirondacks."

Then, when I still remained patiently silent, "I was too upset, however, I suppose; at any rate I went right to bed. When I awoke in the morning, there it was!"

He stopped, as though that were the end of the story.

"What's a heat ray?" I asked. "You've told me everything but something to the point." I indicated the wall with a motion of my head. "What's that?"

He led me over to the window and pointed to one side of the window frame. There was a seared spot.

I scowled at it and bent nearer. "That looks like it's been worked on with a blow torch, too." I looked out. Beyond was a city park. Beneath, was a fifteen foot drop to a cement pavement below. Out in the park a boy and girl—sixteen or seventeen, maybe—were walking along, their arms around each other's waists. Further beyond, hardly discernible, was a cop talking to a baby-carriage-pushing nurse. In a playground to the right, a dozen youngsters played, yelled, and fought.

I turned back to Les Zimmer, who was shaking his head vigorously. "They—*something* hovered over the park, about twenty feet in the air, last night and fired into my room with a heat ray. It came in this window and missed me by inches."

I took that quietly. I went to the wall and pushed the bed out of the way and knelt behind it in front of the burnt area and sighted out the window along the seared place there. It involved sighting slightly upward and over the park. There were no trees right in that vicinity.

I said tonelessly, "You mean from a helicopter or something?"

He laughed in an inane way. "Or *something"* he repeated.

"I stared at the burnt spot on his wall. "You're lucky the house didn't go up."

"Father is a fanatic about fireproofing," he explained. "Almost everything is fireproof; he went to considerable expense to make it that way. The blast must have carried tremendous heat to have made even that much impression on the wall. They must have thought that even if the blast didn't get me, I'd roast in the fire."

I turned back to him again. "All right, here's the sixty-four dollar question. Who are *they?"*

His voice was almost matter of fact. "Why, the aliens."

It had been building up to that, so I wasn't particularly surprised. I looked out the window again at the kids in the playground, the sixteen-year-olds, the cop and the nurse. None of it looked as though there were a Martian stirring. "Let's go down and get some coffee," I told him, and started for the door.

He let me lead the way down the stairs and back through the hall to the kitchen, wordlessly. I tossed my hat to one of the four red chairs that sat around the porcelain-topped table and opened the cupboard to look for the makings. There was both powdered coffee and drip grind.

I said to him, "Can you make coffee?"

"Not very well, but I'll try."

I shook my head emphatically, got out a saucepan and filled it half full of water and put it on the stove. Les got two cups from the cupboard, some spoons and the sugar, and then a can of milk from the refrigerator. His hands were trembling; not that I blamed him.

"Got any liquor?" I asked.

That took a few seconds to sink in, but then he said, "Oh, yes," and went into the dining room through a swinging door at the far end of the kitchen from the hall entrance. I heard a door open and shut in the other room and he returned with a bottle of brandy that looked as though the cork had been drawn out of it months before, but liquid level showed only one or two drinks had been taken. I muttered an inner prayer that the air hadn't got to it.

He set the bottle on the table and I went for the now boiling water. I put a heaping teaspoon of the coffee extract in each of our cups and poured the water on top of it. Then I took the brandy and poured a heavy slug into the first cup.

Zimmer said primly, "I never take stimulants myself, but you are—"

"Today you take stimulants," I snapped back at him. "If I ever saw a guy that needed a drink, it's you."

He didn't say anything more. I gave his cup a good jolt, then sat down. "Now let's get to the point. Suppose you start telling me what you refused to yesterday."

He lifted a spoonful of coffee and blew on it before putting it in his mouth. The spoon made sounds rattling against his teeth. "You mean about—"

"Yeah, exactly. A week ago I'd never even considered the possibility of there being little green men from Mars on—"

He stirred on his chair opposite me. "They wouldn't necessarily be green," he began to protest.

"This is where I came in," I snorted. "All right, I know; for all we know they're purple." I reached into my coat pocket for pipe and tobacco.

He said doggedly, "We haven't the slightest idea what they might look like. Actually, they might be insects, intelligent insects from another world. On the other hand, they might look humanoid like us; or perhaps there is some slight difference in size, or shape, or color." He smiled wanly. "They just might be green."

"There are other possibilities, Mr. Knight. They might be microscopic in size, or invisible to our narrow range of vision. Or they—"

"You've made that point," I said, loading the pipe carefully and tamping the tobacco with my right forefinger. "I'll accept that if there were visitors from space they might look like just about anything. Go on. What evidence is there—if any? Maddigan, Roget and Shulman already gave me that book, *Life on Other Worlds.*"

He nodded seriously. "Don't forget that the author was the Astronomer Royal of England."

"So they told me; half a dozen times, in fact. All right, so this Astronomer Royal thinks that life probably exists on other worlds."

"His opinion isn't lightly to be brushed aside."

"I'll take that, but it's still just an opinion."

"Nor are the so-called flying saucers and kindred phenomena to be ignored."

"Come again?" I said, bringing forth my kitchen matches and lighting up. "What's this about kindred phenomena?"

He finished half his cup of coffee and turned those big serious eyes back to me again. "The things that have been sighted recently weren't all of one type, you know. Most of them were reported to be disc-like in shape, but there were others. Some were cigar-shaped, our usual conception of what a space craft would look like.

"Another point that should be made clear is that the so-called flying saucers aren't anything new."

I interrupted him there. "Wait a minute, now; I thought they were first sighted just a few years ago by some businessmen flying over Washington, or Idaho, or some place in the Northwest."

He nodded. "You're thinking of Kenneth Arnold. But he wasn't the first to sight the flying saucers; he only set off this recent flurry of sightings. Just a minute." Les Zimmer got up from his chair and left the room.

While he was gone, I got up from my own chair and made two more cups of coffee, spiking them both. I could use it, and so could he.

He came back with a heavy book and handed it to me. I looked at the title, *The Books of Charles Fort.* "What's this?" I asked him. "Isn't Fort the screwball that tells all about the rains of frogs and that sort of crap?"

Les Zimmer settled down in his chair again and took another swallow of his coffee. He didn't seem to notice that I'd renewed it, or if he did he wasn't protesting.

"That's hardly a proper description of Charles Fort," he said stiffly, looking down his overgrown nose at me in hauteur—that brandy was doing him a world of good. "Fort has gathered material for decades in an attempt to show that modern science is too smug, too hypocritical—and too ignorant. He made a hobby, a lifetime work, of gathering evidence of phenomena that modern science has as yet been unable to explain."

"Such as what?" I asked skeptically.

"Well, at random, the electrical phenomenon, fireballs—science has no explanation of what they are. Or take these rains of frogs you mentioned. Fort gathered hundreds, if not thousands, of eye witness accounts, sometimes involving absolutely impeccable witnesses, on not only rains of frogs, but of fish, stones, red rain. Science has been unable to explain satisfactorily these happenings, so it usually ignores them."

"Let's forget Fort and his frogs," I protested. "We seem to continually get away from the point."

"My point was that Charles Fort, in gathering his various other material, also gathered accounts of flying saucers that go back over a hundred and fifty years." Les Zimmer shook his head seriously. "The flying saucers aren't a recent development. Kenneth Arnold, the businessman you mentioned, contends that upon research he found records of them that go back to before Christ."

That surprised me. I said, "Kind of knocks out the theory that they're either U.S. or Soviet military craft."

"That's right; they were reported long before the Wright brothers got off the ground," Zimmer said smugly. Most of the shrillness had gone from his voice now. That boy needed to do more good honest drinking.

I digested what he'd said, puffing gently on the brier and sipping at the coffee. "All right, let's go on," I said at last. "How about some other evidence?"

He considered momentarily. "It isn't something that admits of absolute proof, of course. If it did, then we'd all know about it. It's just a matter of adding together a lot of little things."

"Such as?"

With his right hand he made a perplexed motion to the back of his head. "For instance, I read a story not so long ago in which the author developed the idea that snakes and spiders are possibly life forms originally from some other planet."

I set my coffee down at that one.

"You mean that snakes or spiders are capable of building space ships and flying here from, say, Mars?"

He shook his head negatively. "No, of course not. This writer—and its been suggested before—mentions several alternatives. Possibly they are the survivors of an alien space ship that crashed here accidentally hundreds of thousands of years ago. They weren't completely able to adapt themselves to this planet and so degenerated until they are the unintelligent life forms we know today. But the alternative this writer liked best was that they were guinea pigs.

"Guinea pigs?"

"That's right. He suggested that aliens from some other world came to earth thousands of years ago, searching for possible planets for colonization. They landed and left specimens of the lower life forms of their own world here on earth. Their idea was to come back, thousands of years later, to see whether or not the spider and snake had survived. If they were able to survive, then the aliens would deduce that intelligent forms would be able to do the same."

I added another brief shot to my coffee to strengthen it. "Why spiders and snakes?" I asked. "Why should they be aliens?"

Les Zimmer finished his coffee. "Haven't you ever noticed that almost every other animal here on earth is repelled by the very sight of a snake, or a spider? The theory is that instinctively we know that they don't belong; they're alien and our flesh crawls at the sight of them."

My pipe had gone out. I scratched a match on the underside of my chair, lit the tobacco carefully and blew out a long gust of smoke. I sat there, my eyes unseeingly resting on the white door of the refrigerator, considering what he had said thus far. He didn't interrupt me. I said finally, "I suppose you have more of the same—that is, more of this sort of evidence."

He nodded wordlessly.

"But no proof. Just these half-baked ideas, these—"

"No proof stronger than such things as the flying saucers." His tone made the words an objection.

I blew some more smoke around and tried to think, not very successfully. I said, "Was your door locked last night, Les? All of your doors?"

He said, "After I awoke this morning, I checked every door and window in the house. The only one open was that one of mine—my window, I mean. It's at least fifteen feet to the ground."

"Someone could have been down on the sidewalk with a ladder." But even as I said it, I didn't mean it. He would have been spotted by a passing car or a pedestrian too easily.

Zimmer didn't answer me.

I took up a new thread. "Listen, Les, do you know of anyone who would want you dead?"

He didn't get that at first. I said, "Has anybody a motive good enough to kill you?"

"Kill me?"

I was slightly exasperated. "Murder you, I mean. Listen, Les, last night somebody tried to kill you. Whether it was an alien from space, as you call them, or a good old down-to-earth human murderer, the attempt was made. It might be made again. My question is, do you know any *human* who might want to kill you?"

It finally sank in. He sat there wordlessly for a full minute, then got up and made us some more coffee. This time *he* spiked it. He sat down again and stared into his cup. Evidently this aspect of the

matter hadn't even occurred to him. I continued to draw on the
brier, not interrupting. We sipped on the coffee over the next quarter of an hour. Finally he shook his head.

"No. There is no one."

"Almost everybody has someone who'd like to see them dead.
Are you going to inherit any money? Or would anyone inherit any
if you died?"

He laughed bitterly.

"Did you ever steal anybody's girl, or anything else that . . . ?"

He shook his head.

I said, "Listen, Les, there was an attempt on your life last night.
Anything is possible—maybe it *was* extra-terrestrials—but some
things are damn improbable. Chances are, Les, that it was a human. We need a motive. Who would want to kill you; who would
be better off, at least in his mind, if you were dead? Here's an angle that may help you put your finger on the guy: he also wanted
Harry Shulman out of the way. Your would-be murderer is connected with not only you, but Shulman as well. Think hard, Les;
it's your life at stake."

Les Zimmer shook his head again.

I came to my feet. "All right. I guess that's that."

He stared up at me, his prominent eyes going a little wild again.
What should I do, Mr. Knight?"

"Get in touch with the police. Lieutenant Philip Davis at homicide, preferably. Tell him an attempt has been made on your life."

"But—they wouldn't believe my story."

"Brother, you ain't just a-whistlin' Dixie they won't believe
your story. If you want to keep out of the nut factory, you'd better
leave out any part about heat rays and men from space. Just stick
to the facts."

"You mean that they might send me to an asylum?" His earnest
eyes were wide now.

"The authorities seem to take a dim view of people who even
see flying saucers and little men; I don't know what they'd do to
someone who claimed these Martians were out to get him."

I put my pipe back into my pocket, feeling its warmth through
the cloth. "It might be a good idea, too," I told him, "if you didn't
mention ringing me in on the situation. Davis already knows I'm
working on this phase of the question; if he knew you'd spent a
couple of hours telling me about it first, he might have you in a
strait-jacket before you knew what was going on."

He took me to the front door. I noticed that he went through the same rigmarole as when I'd entered. Before opening up he carefully peered through the curtain to see if the road was clear.

"Get in touch with me if anything else comes up," I told him in parting.

He muttered something I didn't catch.

CHAPTER TEN

IT WAS GETTING to the point where I thought that if I didn't talk to somebody at least semi-normal I'd develop a leak in my own roof. I walked down toward Montgomery Boulevard from Zimmer's house, trying to put my finger on just who that might be. My impression of most of the characters I was coming in contact with led me to the uncomfortable feeling that I was dealing with a group of mental jitterbugs.

I stood on the corner of Montgomery, theoretically waiting for a cab, actually gazing, more or less unthinkingly, at the cars whizzing by. A Ford, a Chevvy, a Ford, a Buick, a Pontiac, a Dodge, a Nash, a Chevvy, a Plymouth, a Kaiser, some make I didn't recognize—when I was a kid I knew them all—a Ford, a midget Crosley, a Chevvy.

A cab stopped finally, without my having hailed it. The driver stuck his head through the window and started to say, "Cab, mis . . ." He recognized me and finished off with, "You wouldn't want to be going a block or two, would you?" It was my driver of the day before.

I didn't have the gumption to growl at him. I got in the back silently.

He flipped down his flag and whined, "Where to?"

"Just a minute," I told him; "let me think."

"Take your time, buddy. It all adds up if we go or not."

Finally I got my list out of my pocket and ran a finger down it indecisively. What I was doing in this business was a mystery even bigger than the one confronting me. Some investigator! Good old Jeb Custer Knight, super sleuth!

I read off an address to him and told myself I'd spend the time it'd take to get there trying to piece together some odds and ends that *must* make some sense if assembled correctly. They didn't. I assembled them this way, that way, and the other way, like a kid with blocks. Perhaps I didn't have the right odds and ends. This was strictly fertilizer for the aviary.

The cabby pulled up before the home of Ross Maddigan about a quarter of an hour later, and I piled out and paid him. He shot into low gear and was off.

I looked up at the house for a full minute, then, on a sudden intuition, went up the neatly graveled walk and, instead of continuing up the brick steps to the door, cut around the side toward the hedged garden in the rear. The hedge, in the light of day, didn't seem as heavy as I had remembered it. I ended up beneath the large tree whose limbs had shaded Harry Shulman's dead body. A few of them, heavy and gnarled, extended over the hedge itself.

I could hear a typewriter clicking in the garden. Parting my way through the hedge, I stuck my head inside, coming up face to face with Ross Maddigan.

He was about ten feet away, dressed in shorts and sandals, nothing else, and was sitting before a substantial-looking card table which supported a portable typewriter. He had several different piles of paper on the table, a dictionary, another heavy book which was probably a thesaurus, and a multitude of pencils, pens, paper clips and erasers.

He said, "Hello," his eyes widening slightly.

I grinned at him. "Didn't want to startle you, but I thought I'd get a load of this set-up during the day. I was going to come around front and ring the bell in a minute, but when I heard your typewriter . . ."

"Oh, sure," he said. "Come on in, Jeb."

I wedged myself the rest of the way through, then looked back reflectively. "It isn't hard getting through that hedge."

Ross came to his feet to shake hands with me. The day was hot and sultry, but his hand was still dry and firm. He admitted the hedge was no Siegfried Line. "As a matter of fact," he said, "there are even easier spots than where you came through. I think Lieutenant Davis has already considered the possibility that Harry was taken outside to be killed, then returned. Come on into the house; we'll have a beer."

I should have said something to the effect that I didn't need a beer, that I'd been slopping up coffee royal for the past couple of hours, but it sounded good to me, and besides, the sun was too emphatic about things out there on the garden lawn. I could use some shade. I followed him wordlessly.

Ross Maddigan's overgrown refrigerator was as well stocked as ever. He located two bottles of Blatz, beads of cold sweat on their sides, and put them on the table.

Ross said, "Like a sandwich? I've still got a lot of cold cuts left over from the party the other night. There's ham, cheese, liverwurst, salami—"

"All right, thanks; I could use a sandwich," I admitted.

He went over to the cupboard and got a gigantic loaf of pumpernickel bread, a small jar of mustard and a couple of knives. He kept the conversation going while he built up the sandwiches and opened the beer.

"Julie says you saw her yesterday. How about ham and cheese, kind of a Dagwood?"

I nodded yes to both.

"I didn't quite get it when you phoned for her address. That morning you'd turned me down when I wanted you to work on Harry's death; then, later, you said you'd taken the case, evidently with another client."

I was hungrily eyeing the sandwich he was making, beginning to realize that I'd been doing too much drinking the last few days and not nearly enough eating. I told him, "I didn't take on the job of finding a murderer—not exactly, at least. Art Roget and your uncle hired me to continue the investigation into the possibilities of there being extra-terrestrials on earth. They thought Shulman might have been killed to cover over their presence."

He finished the sandwiches, put them on saucers and slid one over to me. It must have weighed all of a pound and a half. Then he took up a can opener and with the bottle opener end popped the tops off the beer bottles. He poured the cold beer into two tall glasses, tall enough to take the full contents.

"I thought that was a gag for the convention," he said, taking a huge bite.

I followed his example. "So did I," I told him around the chewing, "but your uncle and Roget came around and twisted my arm. Listen, Ross, I'm in business. If they want to hire me to look for aliens from space, who am I to argue?" There was probably a defensive tone in my voice.

He was frowning, an expression out of place on his easygoing face. "I see *your* point," he said slowly, "but I can't see my uncle financing the project."

I lifted my right shoulder in a shrug. "Usually kind of careful with his money, uh? Well, you're right; as soon as he thought the idea over a mite he canceled it."

Ross's frown deepened. "How do you mean? You're still working for him."

"He called this morning and told me he and Art had decided to call it off as soon as my retainer is used up. I'm to work two more days. I guess when the excitement of the killing wore off, he began to see some of the more obvious angles. Besides, Zimmer went over and gave him and Roget the devil for laying you fans open to ridicule."

He took another bite of his sandwich. "Oh, Les, eh?"

There didn't seem to be any answer to that beyond a nod. I said, "Thing is that Les Zimmer talked your uncle out of the project last night, but he's all keen for it this morning."

"Les is?" Ross Maddigan was chewing industriously and with obvious relish—no wonder he weighed nearly two hundred, if he considered this just a between meals snack. His eyebrows were up questioningly.

"Yeah," I said. "By the way, what is a heat ray? I never did find out."

"A heat ray? I don't know. When science fiction writers are trying to dream up some kind of gobbledy-gook weapon that's used in the future or on Mars or Venus, or wherever, they sometimes call it a heat ray."

I stopped chewing for a minute and rinsed down my mouthful of pumpernickel, cheese and ham with a swallow of the beer. I said, "Then nobody here on earth has one?"

Ross looked as though he didn't know what this had to do with the conversation, but he said, "I think I read somewhere that the Japs had been experimenting with a heat ray during the war, but that the best they could do was kill a canary at a distance of about fifteen feet. Why?"

I took another bite of my sandwich. "Somebody took a shot at Les Zimmer with one last night. Burned the bejazus out of the wall just beyond his bed and missed him by only a few inches. Looked as though the ray were beamed right through his window."

Ross Maddigan put his sandwich down and stared at me.

I shrugged. "That's the way it looks, Ross. I was just over there. Don't tell me I'm nuts; I already know it. So is everything else that's been going on for the past few days."

Ross finished up his glass of beer without taking his eyes from me, then got up and went over to the icebox for another couple of bottles. He opened them and put mine before me so that I could pour my own. He still looked dumbfounded.

I said, "Don't ask me if I'm sure; I'm not sure of anything any more. I came over here because you're the nearest thing to a sane person I've run into on this case—you and Julie; everybody else seems to be halfway around the corner."

He said slowly, "Harry Shulman and now Les Zimmer."

I nodded. "One of the things I wanted to ask you, Ross: Is there any connection between those two boys that might call for somebody wanting to kill them both? Some motive that might apply to—"

He was already shaking his head. "They knew each other—but none too well. I think they put out a little fanzine together a few years ago. But otherwise—"

"They didn't work in the same office, or date the same girls or have any other connections outside science fiction?"

He still shook his head. "Harry was a fountain manager at some drug store or other; Les works in a print shop. In fact, he has a small press in his cellar; does up our programs and so forth."

"I've seen it."

"But I would say that aside from the Scylla Club and science fiction, they have practically nothing in common."

"Except both of them were more than usually convinced that there were possibly aliens on earth today."

Ross moved his lips, making his mouth small. "Well, Harry didn't particularly tend in that direction, but Les certainly does."

"Oh? I picked up the impression that Harry made quite a hobby of it. But anyway, who else around here—if anybody—thinks the same thing?"

He had gone back to his sandwich again, thoughtfully now, eating absently and taking an occasional swig of the beer. "I can't think of anyone in particular in this city; a fan named Bob Carr, out in Indianapolis, is the one who's really gone overboard on the subject. He's written a score of articles for the fanzines on alien life on earth. Of course—"

Ross Maddigan had hesitated, so I prompted him. "Of course, what?"

He stirred uncomfortably. "Well, most of us have a certain amount of interest in the subject and believe in alien life to varying degrees."

I closed my eyes and groaned, "Oh, my aching back. Not you, too!"

Ross tried a short laugh. "I said in varying degrees. For instance—" He got to his feet and left the room for a minute to return with a book. "This is *Conquest of Space* by Willy Ley," he told me. "It isn't fiction, and Willy Ley is possibly the outstanding authority on space travel and related subjects."

"I think Art Roget mentioned him that first day they came to my office."

"Very possibly. At any rate, listen to this . . ." He leafed through pages for a minute, found his passage and read, ". . . *We are justified in believing in life on Mars—hardy plant life. The color changes which we can see are explained most logically and most simply by assuming vegetation.*" He skipped some lines, then went on, *"Of terrestrial plants, lichen might survive transplanting to Mars and one may imagine that some of the desert flora of Tibet could be adapted. At any event conditions are such that life as we know it would find the going tough, but not impossible."*

"All right," I nodded, "what's the point?"

"The point is," he said, closing the book and tossing it to the table, "that you don't have to be a crackpot to believe that life exists on other planets, and possibly other star systems."

"Listen, now, wait a minute," I protested. "This guy's talking about plant life, lichens, for instance; not about little green men that go around mashing people or firing heat rays at them."

He finished the rest of the beer in his glass and poured more before answering me. Then he said, "You don't get it, Jeb. Can't you see that if you admit there's any life at all, besides on the earth, you've admitted the greatest part of it? If plant life can exist elsewhere, then the possibility, if not the probability, is that higher life has evolved also."

I didn't answer that. After taking the time to think it over, I dropped it to go on to another angle. "Let me put it to you this way, Ross," I said.

"Fire away." He looked over at the loaf of pumpernickel calculatingly, evidently wondering whether or not to make another sandwich.

I said, "Harry Shulman has been killed and Les Zimmer narrowly escaped death. Do you believe it was done by extra-terrestrials?"

Ross picked up a small piece of bread that had dropped from his sandwich to his plate and crumbled it in his fingers. He shook his head negatively. "No, I don't," he said.

"All right, why don't you? The only motive we seem to have is that these two were both suspicious of such aliens."

"No," he said, making an impatient gesture. Then: "Jeb, it's all very fine gathering this evidence about extra-terrestrials. It's fun considering the possibility of their existence; what they'd look like, what they'd think like, what they'd think of us, whether or not it would be possible to communicate with them—all the rest of it. The whole thing is interesting.

"But, Jeb, when it comes to cold-blooded murder—like the death of poor little Harry Shulman out there in my garden—I say *no*. Maybe I'm wrong, but I'd lay every cent I've got on a human killer, not an extraterrestrial one."

I finished off the last signs of sandwich and beer silently. I couldn't think of anything else, off hand, to ask him. When they were gone I came to my feet with a sigh.

"You're working," I told him. "I'll get along."

He leaned back on the back legs of the chair and stuck his hands in the pockets of his shorts. "Don't worry about that. I'm through for the day now. One bottle of beer I can get away with, but if I drink two, somehow or other the day's shot. I won't be able to write any more."

I asked him, "There isn't anything else you can think of that might help me, is there?"

"No. Afraid not."

I took my list of names from my pocket and handed it to him. "Art Roget gave me a list of those present the other night. Do you think that any of them in particular could help me out?"

He ran his eyes down the list thoughtfully. Finally he looked up and said, "I don't know what to tell you, Jeb. If you're still working on the slant of alien life forms here on earth, I doubt if any of these people could tell you any more than Les Zimmer, or even I, could. If you're thinking in terms of a human murderer, well, frankly, I can't see why any of these would want to see Harry out of the way. Aside from their contact with him through the club, none of them had any connection with him, or any real interest in him. Not as far as I know, and I think I would know."

I took the list back and stuck it in my pocket.

"Just one other thing," I said. "Have you considered the possibility that Harry was killed by mistake? That someone else was intended to be the victim? Have you considered that possibly Harry inadvertently took *your* place?"

He looked up at me. "Sure, I've considered it, especially when the police could find no motive for Harry's death. But how does that tie in with the attempt on Les? Did this mysterious person who thought he was killing me when he got Harry also think that I was sleeping in Les Zimmer's bed last night?"

He tossed the idea off. "Besides, there isn't any more motive for killing me than there is for either of the others. I'm just an un-reconstructed vet who's making an unsuccessful attempt to break into the writing game. I haven't any enemies, not much money,

I'm engaged to the woman I love and, as far as I know, nobody is trying to take her away from me."

"Hold it there," I grinned at him. "Maybe we've found a motive in this whole crazy case at last."

Ross Maddigan grinned back, ruefully. "She's wonderful, isn't she?"

I told him yeah, and picked up my hat from where I'd tossed it in an empty chair.

We said goodbye and shook hands again—he seemed a regular demon for shaking hands—and I took off, out the front door this time instead of through the hedge.

He stood at the entrance behind me, and called another cheery goodbye and an invitation to drop around any time.

A good joe.

~ ~ ~ ~ ~

At the end of the gravel walk I looked first at my watch and then at my list of names. Ross Maddigan hadn't helped me much there. He hadn't even been able to think of anyone worth talking to— neither could I.

There was a streetcar stop two blocks down. I started walking and trying to figure out the next step. It was late afternoon; half or more of the names I had would be at work. I looked at the list again and it hit me whom I wanted to see next.

James Maddigan would be at work. If I wanted to see Sandra, away from him, this would be the time of day to do it. I still couldn't make her out. I couldn't get the angle of her coming up to the office the day before. Ross Maddigan, yes; I could see why he'd want to be sure that the person who killed a friend in his garden was found and proven guilty. But Sandra? She'd admitted that she didn't even know Harry Shulman, or at least not more than to say hello.

Obviously, Sandra was my next point of call. Besides, the address indicated that she was within a mile or so.

I wished that I hadn't lapped up so much liquor so early in the day. It was beginning to die in me.

CHAPTER ELEVEN

I WAS PREPARED to find the James Maddigans living in a comfortable home, considering that Ross wasn't exactly poverty-stricken and that both Sandra and her husband dressed as though they were to the manner born. But I wasn't prepared for the ultra luxury of their hotel apartment.

An impeccably dressed jerk at the desk of the Marion Arms eyed me superciliously, asked for my name and pursed his lips before condescending to phone up to the Maddigan apartment.

Evidently Sandra Maddigan was at home and evidently she told him to hustle me through. The supercilious look blended into a leer which I didn't get at the time.

The elevator smoothed me up to the fourteenth floor, and I didn't have to take the time to look about for Apartment 1400, because there was Sandra, coming down the hall toward me, her hands extended happily as though I were a husband just back from the wars. The elevator boy's face was impassive. I wouldn't lose any money betting that he'd been through this scene before.

"Jeb!" she gushed, "I'm so pleased to see you. I was afraid that you were angry with little Sandra." She pouted, but I still didn't like women who pout, not even when they had the lush, full mouth of a Sandra Maddigan.

She was wearing a colorful housecoat which couldn't possibly have cost as much as you estimated. But for that matter, it seemed equally impossible that that many yards of cloth could do so much in the way of indicating what lay below.

She took me by the arm happily and walked me back to the apartment, bubbling along as we went. I didn't get it.

The Maddigan apartment was about as far out of my class as you can get. Its terrace reached out above a clever patio below; its six or eight rooms ran off in all directions from the tremendous living room. The furniture was striking without being uncomfortable; modern without being Hollywoodish. Whoever had decorated the Maddigan apartment—and it could have been neither James nor Sandra—had been paid, but plenty.

I pursed my lips and whistled softly. "I thought science fiction fans were inclined to be along the proletarian side."

She shrugged, pouting again, "Don't be snobbish. If you have money, why not spend it?"

"Yeah," I said, "why not?"

There must have been servants around somewhere, but I didn't see them. When the clerk announced me, she had evidently been sitting on a couch reading. A book lay face down; nearby was a tray complete with a tall impressive-looking bottle, an ice bucket and a bottle of soda. I noted the title of the book, *Male and Female,* by Jack Woodford. I murmured inwardly, "Imagine a dame that looks like this having to *read* about it." There was a double row of additional books in a low bookcase to one side of the couch—detective and love novels.

She plumped down on the couch and patted the place beside her and immediately reached for the bottle.

I said suspiciously, "What's that?"

"Metaxa," she beamed. "Best brandy in the *world,* you know; comes from Greece. Do sit down, Jeb." She expertly made drinks and I figured that either Greek brandy wasn't as strong as cognac or that she was really socking it to us. I lowered myself gingerly to the couch beside her.

She went on, "It really should be taken straight, but when I get tied up in a book, I like to drink as I go along, and if you're drinking straight you get tight too soon. Don't you think?"

I wasn't following her very well, but I said, "Yes."

She handed me one of the tall glasses, sank back into the couch and said, "So you changed your mind." I was beginning to wonder if she'd deliberately cultivated that pout to emphasize the sexiness of her lower lip.

"How was that?" I asked her.

"You've decided to work for me after all."

"Not exactly, Mrs. Maddigan," I said.

"Sandra."

"All right, Sandra. I've got another client; I'm working on a different aspect of the case. I just thought I'd drop in and see if you could help me on one or two points."

Sandra Maddigan took a sip of her drink, still eyeing me; I took a gulp of mine.

She reached over a well manicured hand and felt my arm. Her fingernails dug in. "Lord, it's good to feel a man's arm that has muscles in it for a change." She leaned back against the couch. "It's good to even talk to a *man.*"

I took another gulp of the Metaxa. It was strong enough to stand by itself. "Thanks," I said. "Where'd you get the idea I was such a chunk of masculinity? Actually, I like my steaks medium well—"

She looked me over again. "You wouldn't be in the business you are unless you craved a real man's life. Excitement, trouble, adventure." She shivered. "Tell me about it; I've never known a detective before."

"Tell you about the detective game? You wouldn't believe me if I did. It's not what you think; you've been reading novels, or maybe seeing William Powell in the movies."

I'd got the answer I was looking for when I came up here to see Sandra. The day before I'd wondered why she had come to my office—the real reason, that is.

Now I knew. She'd never "met" a private detective before.

I reached over, picked up the bottle of Metaxa, and poured myself a quick shot. I took it down with a single, stiff-wristed motion, and got to my feet. She stared up at me in surprise.

"Listen," I said thickly, "I'm supposed to be working. We'll have to put this off until another time. I came here to ask a couple of questions; I already know the answer to one of them."

Over her face chased surprise, impatience, chagrin and anger in a space of a few seconds. She snapped, "What questions? Do you mean you're going to leave me like this?"

"Like what?" I said impatiently.

She flushed angrily behind what was left of her makeup, took up her glass and finished it off, and changed the subject. "What do you mean, *questions?*" Her voice was shaky.

I said, "You're no more interested in science fiction than I am. What was your real reason for going to Ross's party the other night?"

Her eyes blazed furiously.

Suddenly, without her speaking, I knew the answer to that one too. In my mind's eye Ross's wide-open, honest face swam into view. I recalled something I'd forgotten that night in the garden when Harry Shulman had died. I remembered a brief scene where Sandra stood close to him, her hand on Ross's arm, and he looking red about the gills with embarrassment.

"All right, never mind the questions," I told her, trying to keep disgust from my voice.

Sandra's face suddenly went soft again. She came to her feet and put her hand on my arm. "I'm so tired, Jeb; and really those awful policemen questioned me forever. How about calling it off until some other time? I might say something I shouldn't; you wouldn't want to take advantage of me." Her mouth smiled, and raw sex peered out of her eyes.

"I don't think I'd be up to that," I murmured, looking around for my hat. I wondered vaguely why she didn't want me to ask her any questions; I couldn't think of anything she could possibly know that might be to the point. I was a helluva investigator, I was.

She saw me to the door, pouting again now. While I was putting on my hat, she reached up and felt my arm again. Her eyes narrowed sensually.

"You still look like quite a bit of man to me, and I still think being a detective must be a hard, tough racket."

I put my forefinger under her chin, and dropped a quick peck of a kiss on her lips. "No tougher than landing a rich man for a husband, and then hanging on in spite of the fact that you can't stand the sight of him."

CHAPTER TWELVE

I COULD HEAR the phone ringing as I came down the corridor from the elevator the next morning. I zipped the key into the lock, to the extent I was capable of zipping, which wasn't very much, and hurried open the door.

The phone started complaining shrilly again, so I picked it up and said, "Jeb Knight."

A voice told me, "This is James Maddigan, Knight. Did you send in your report as yet?"

I said, "Yeah, it's in the mail. Have you heard about what happened to Les Zimmer?"

Maddigan didn't sound particularly interested, but he said, "Zimmer? No, what?"

I hesitated, then said, "It'd take too long to tell you over the phone. The report should be there in the morning delivery."

"Very well," he said. "Are you to attend the convention today?"

I'd forgotten that this was the first day of the science fiction convention. "Did you want me to?" I asked him.

He hesitated again. "Well, this is the last day that you'll be working for Arthur Roget and me, but since you're already at the task and have been remunerated for it, I think the convention might offer you as suitable an opportunity as any to further investigate this matter."

"All right, you're the boss," I told him. "The convention it is. When and where does it start?"

"The local fan clubs have rented the auditorium of Sherman Halls. Are you familiar with its location?"

"Next to the Bigelow Hotel, isn't it? Same management as the Bigelow, in fact."

"That is correct. The convention is officially to begin at noon, but I imagine the fen are beginning to gather even now."

There was a shadow at my door, a bulky shadow that I seemed to recognize.

I asked, "Are you going to be there, Mr. Maddigan?"

"Not today. The convention will continue four days in all. I shall have to be present at the office this initial one so that I may attend tomorrow and the ensuing days. I shall probably be there late tonight, however."

"All right," I told him, cutting it short; the knob was beginning to turn on the door. "I'll see you later."

We hung up, just as Sergeant Mike Quinn came in the door. Up to and including the unlit cigar in his face, he looked identically the same as he had the day before.

I sighed—perhaps it should be called a groan—and said, "Good morning, Sergeant."

He grinned at me. "Now that's a matter of opinion, Buster. I wonder if you'll think so after you've seen the lieutenant."

"What?" I protested. "Again?"

He nodded cheerfully. "Again. The lieutenant understands that you had a busy little time for yourself after you left headquarters yesterday."

I got up in resignation and reached over for my hat. Dust on the windowsill had added a dirtier than usual tinge to the brim. I flicked it against my leg a couple of times before donning it. "You know," I said petulantly, "theoretically I don't have to come unless I'm under arrest."

"It's a beautiful theory, but you'd be surprised how it works out in actual practice. Wanta try, Buster?"

I shook my head. "Let's go."

As I closed the door behind us, he said, "Who was that on the phone, your grandmother again?"

I nodded. I wasn't up to the banter Quinn liked.

The same bored, expressionless cop sat in what could have been and probably was the same car that they'd picked me up in the day before. We climbed into the back and took off up Marion to East First and north on East First to Lafayette. The Justice Building hadn't changed any in the past twenty-four hours either; we sped up its wide driveway to the rear, climbed out and worked our way up the steps to the second floor.

I made a feeble try at humor. "I'd hate for this to become a habit," I told Quinn. "For one thing, that jet plane test-pilot you use for a driver—"

He grunted, "That's up to you, shamus."

"Aw, no," I protested in pain. "Not you too. Listen, I've been explaining all week that nobody ever calls anybody a shamus except in stories."

"Talking about stories," he muttered, "you better have a good one for the lieutenant. That's in the way of advice; he ain't in any too good a humor, Buster."

"Not doing so well on the case, eh?"

He glowered at me. "That ain't what I said."

At the door lettered *Lieutenant Davis, Homicide Detail,* we knocked and walked in. Davis was sitting behind his desk as though he hadn't moved since I saw him last. He still looked like a white grub who'd crawled out from under some log.

He took his feet down from off the desk blotter, stuck them where they belonged and stared at me unblinkingly.

I sighed, looked around for a chair, located one and pulled it over and sat down. I mustered as nonchalant a face as I could and waited for him to start in.

Mike Quinn leaned back against the wall, grinning. He opened his mouth to say something, and Davis snapped, "Shut up, Mike."

Sergeant Quinn looked aggrieved.

"You didn't bother to listen to what I had to say yesterday, eh?" Davis growled at me. He wasn't looking for an answer yet, so I kept quiet.

"You left here and, like a wise guy, shook your tail. If he hadn't been as much of an amateur as you are, you couldn't have done it, but you did. You shook him and then spent the day messing in police affairs."

I started to say something then, but he held up a thin, bony hand. "First of all, what was the big idea telling that Zimmer kid not to tell us you'd been there, eh?"

I lifted my right shoulder and let it drop. "Listen, Lieutenant, you told me you didn't want me to interfere in your murder case. All right. It's not my fault if Les Zimmer phones me before he does you. As soon as I found out what he had called me for, I told him to get in touch with your office. No use getting you upset, so I told him not to mention I'd been there."

"What did you foul up before I arrived?" he growled.

"Not a thing. We went into the kitchen and chewed the rag a while about visitors from space . . ."

"Oh, brother," Quinn laughed.

"Shut up, Mike," Davis snapped, shooting him an irritated glance. "So you're still sounding off about that, eh?" he went on to me.

"Listen," I said, complaint in my voice. "I told you what the deal was. As a matter of fact, this is my last day on it; Maddigan and Roget have decided to call my investigation off."

"It'd better be," Davis snapped. "What else did you do yesterday?"

"Crying out loud, do you want it all? I got up in the morning with a hangover and had corn flakes and milk for breakfast. Then I—"

"Don't get smart with me, wise guy." His colorless eyes narrowed and he drummed his thin fingers on the desk in irritation. "Who else did you see, eh?"

I said patiently, "I keep telling you this is another matter. I talked with Sandra and Ross Maddigan."

"About men from Mars, eh?"

"About extra-terrestrials—mostly."

Davis grunted with impatience and seemed to be considering inwardly whether or not to ask this next question. Finally he said, "When you were at the Shulman house, day before yesterday, did you take anything? Were you in the cellar?"

"What are you talking about?" I said.

"Forget it," Davis said. He sat there in silence; his eyes left me to go to the dirty window and off into the distance as he thought his thoughts. Finally he shifted in his chair and said, "What d'ya think happened over there at Zimmer's? That burn in the wall."

I took a deep breath and said deliberately, "It looks as though some extra-terrestrial took a shot at him with a heat ray."

Davis remained silent for at least thirty seconds; then he snapped, "You get the hell out of here, Knight." There were spots of red in his shrunken cheeks.

I came to my feet. "All right," I said mildly. "I didn't want to come in the first place."

"You're a little bit too snotty for your own good," he growled. "We'll see where it gets you, wise guy."

I turned and walked out, closing the door behind me. They watched silently as I went, anger on Davis's face, amusement on Quinn's.

Instead of turning to the right to leave the building I crossed the corridor and took my time getting a drink from the battered water cooler there. No one had followed me, so I turned left and walked quickly thirty or forty feet to another door lettered simply, *Homicide.*

I opened the door and stuck my head in. Hermie Cain was sitting alone at a desk, reading a true detective magazine, and radiating boredom. He looked up at my entrance.

"Hi, Jeb," he said. "Come on in; how're ya?"

I told him all right and he tossed his magazine to the desk and leaned back to gab.

"Listen," I said, "I'd like to chew the rag a while but I'm in kind of a hurry. I wanted to ask you something."

"Good enough; ask me," he yawned. Momentarily, I could see him the way he'd been four years ago in a khaki instead of a blue uniform; indolent except for those times when temper would boil over and he'd spend twenty minutes roaring about the army's way of operating. Usually Hermie could be found goofing off somewhere, yawning and complaining that he didn't get enough sleep. He slept more than any other three men in the company.

"Hermie," I asked him, "what turned up missing at the Shulman house?"

He scowled. "Shulman house?"

"You know, that killing Davis is on. Harry Shulman."

"Oh," he was still scowling, "dammit, Jeb, you know I'm not supposed—" He broke off and scratched his chin in irritation. "The old lady phoned in and said that burglars had swiped something or other."

I leaned forward, resting my hands on the desk before him. "What?"

"I'll be hanged if I remember. It was some magazines or something."

I growled, "A lot of good you do me." I straightened up. "Well, thanks anyway. See you later, Hermie."

He yawned and picked up his magazine again when he saw I was about to go. "Good enough, Jeb." He sneered at the magazine. "If this isn't the damnedest tripe," he complained. But his head was buried in it as I left.

There was a pay booth at the end of the corridor. I walked down to it, fishing in my pocket for a nickel. The phone book hung outside and I opened it, located the S section and ran my finger down to the Shulmans. There it was, listed under his name, Harold Shulman.

I went into the booth, closing the door carefully, dropped my nickel and dialed the number.

I could see her in my mind's eye coming down the hall from the kitchen, wiping her thin hands on her apron.

Her voice said, "Hello."

I said, "Mrs. Shulman, this is Jeb Knight. You'll remember that I was at your home the other day talking about Harry."

She didn't answer for a moment; then she said hesitatingly, "Yes, yes, I remember. Later, the police officers told me that you weren't a real policeman at all."

"I didn't tell you that I was, Mrs. Shulman. I told you that I was a detective. I'm a private detective."

"I don't know about such things. The officers said I didn't really have to talk to you at all."

"Of course not, Mrs. Shulman." I tried to keep impatience from my voice. "But I *am* trying to help, to find some reason for this tragedy."

There was weariness in her voice. "Why did you call, Mr. Knight?"

I got to the point. "I understand that something of Harry's has been taken from the house."

"Oh." She hesitated again. "The officers said—"

"Certainly, Mrs. Shulman. If you don't wish to tell me about it, you don't have to."

"Well, I can't see that it could do any harm. Harry's magazines are gone."

I scowled. "What magazines?"

"The little magazine he mimeographed. He used to distribute it to the other science fiction fans, you know. He called it, let me see—"

"*Off-Trail Fantasy?*" I suggested, feeling a tightening in my throat.

"That's right. He was very serious about it, you know. He had the latest issue—he brought them out irregularly, not on time every month—all ready to mail, down there in his little space in the cellar. Now they're all gone. I don't see . . ."

I didn't get this at all.

"How do you mean, gone? You mean they've been stolen?"

"I was about to say that I can't understand *how* they could be gone."

"Mrs. Shulman, are you sure he didn't mail them before the tragedy?"

"Yes, I'm sure. He had just finished stapling them together that day, before he went to the party. I think he took just one copy with him."

"Yes, I know," I said softly. My lips were dry; I wet them with my tongue. "Mrs. Shulman, is anything else gone? Is it possible that a burglar—" The question sounded silly to me, even as I asked it.

"No—nothing else."

I talked to her for a few more minutes, getting nothing. She always locked her door when she left the house. No, none of the other fans had a key. No, she hadn't read the issue. No, she couldn't imagine why anyone would want it.

I thanked her and hung up.

I looked at my watch. It still wasn't quite noon. I had plenty of time to get over to Sherman Halls and the convention.

I walked back to the office of *Lee and Knight, Private Investigations,* trying to make sense out of somebody stealing Harry Shulman's latest issue of *Off-Trail Fantasy.*

The elevator growled me up to my floor and I unlocked the office door and, not taking time to close it after me, strode over to the desk. There was only one way that the theft made sense. Harry had evidently run something in that issue that somebody was keen on keeping quiet. Keen enough to kill the boy, keen enough to burgle his house of the copies he'd been on the verge of mailing.

I opened the top desk drawer and flicked through the odds and ends of papers there. It wasn't there. I hurriedly went through the other drawers, trying to remember which one I'd tossed it into. It made no difference; it wasn't in any of them.

I slumped down into my chair and stared at the worn green blotter on the desk surface, and pictured the scene in my mind. I'd come to the office that morning after the Scylla Club party with a sizzling hangover and a bottle to help kill it. The magazine had been uncomfortably bulky in my pocket so I'd thrown it into— yes, into the second drawer. Shortly after, I'd been visited in turn by Ross Maddigan, Sandra Maddigan, then Art Roget and James Maddigan.

I tried to remember whether or not the drawer had been open while any of them had been present. No, it hadn't been. I was sure of that. I tried to remember whether or not I'd mentioned having the magazine to any of them. I was sure I hadn't.

To my knowledge, no one knew I had a copy of the latest issue of *Off-Trail Fantasy.* No one at all. When Harry Shulman had taken me to the side at the party and told me about it, asking me to read it, no one had seen it change hands.

In short, as far as I knew, no one had been aware that I had the copy. But it was gone. Just as gone as the stack in his cellar.

I got up from the swivel chair, walked up and down the tiny room twice, and stared out from the window for a full ten minutes. The dismal view must have been the same as ever, but I didn't notice it. I turned back to the desk and opened the drawer for a pipe. I filled it from the pound tin and sat down again.

For the past few days I'd been chasing around talking to people, talking and talking, and learning nothing of value. Now here was something I should be able to tie into.

I picked up the phone and dialed Maddigan's business number. A feminine voice answered, "Maddigan and Maddigan."

I said, "Is James Maddigan there?"

"One moment, please."

I waited my moment, and then an impatient voice rumbled, "Yes. This is Maddigan."

"Jeb Knight," I said.

"Yes? I thought you were to attend the convention."

"Something came up. Listen, did you get that little magazine that Harry Shulman used to put out?"

"I was unaware he printed one. You mean a fanzine?" His voice had a far away sound, as though he weren't particularly concentrating on what I was saying.

"That's right," I told him. "It was called *Off-Trail Fantasy.*"

"Oh, yes. I do recall now. No, I didn't subscribe. As a matter of fact, I didn't really know Harry very well, you realize. Until we were both elected to the convention entertainment committee I hardly knew him more than to exchange greetings. Why do you ask?"

"The whole issue has disappeared."

His voice was puzzled. "I don't believe I understand you."

"It looks as though somebody has stolen the current issue of *Off-Trail Fantasy.*"

"Why?" I had his attention now, but his voice was still puzzled.

"I don't know why. I was at Lieutenant Davis's office a short time ago and he let drop a hint. I checked with a friend of mine at headquarters and finally wiggled it out."

Maddigan said, "It doesn't seem to make sense. At any rate, write it up in your report tonight. I'm exceedingly busy now, Knight. But tell me, do the police seem to be achieving progress in their endeavors? Have they as yet found their motive for Harry's death?"

"I don't think so. Nor for the attempt on Zimmer, either. I suppose you read about Les Zimmer and his heat ray in the report I sent you last night."

"Yes, I did. Quite fantastic. Well, Knight, suppose you cover the convention today and see if you can come upon anything there. Your employment, of course, will expire tonight. Let me see, we shall still owe you something for expenses."

"A few dollars for taxis is all. I'll bill you for it."

"Very well, Mr. Knight. Good day."

We hung up and I sat there staring at the phone. Finally I picked up the phone book from its spot on the left corner of the desk and looked up Ross Maddigan's number. I dialed him, but there was no answer. He was probably either already at the Sherman Halls auditorium, or on his way.

Just for luck, I searched through the desk again, particularly the second drawer. It wasn't there.

CHAPTER THIRTEEN

I T WAS HIGH TIME that I get over to the convention, but I'd had only coffee for breakfast and I needed something on my stomach before undergoing that ordeal, something hot and somesomething substantial. I left the office and walked over to the corner of Marion and Herkimer to the Acme Lunch, the neighborhood dirty spoon. I got a large bowl of beef stew and approximately half a pound of semi-stale white bread.

The first few mouthfuls were hard getting down, but from there on it wasn't too bad. I finished with more of an appetite than when I'd started. I told myself it was going to be a long time before I had another drink.

I sat at the table picking my teeth and messing with a second cup of coffee until the waitress started hovering over me. Well, it couldn't be put off indefinitely. I got to my feet, slipped a fifteen-cent tip under a saucer, paid the bill, and returned to the street. The summer heat was with us in earnest; I squinted against the sun and felt my shirt stick to my back. I squared my shoulders and bravely set off for the AnnCon, the tenth anniversary of the World Science Fiction Convention.

I walked over to city center and got a Stark Avenue bus running south. Sherman Halls and the Bigelow Hotel were located at Morgan Avenue and East Tenth; I got off at Morgan and Eighth and walked over to Tenth. I stood there for a moment, looking up at the building. I'd never been inside, but I knew they had at least a half-dozen halls of various sizes, from an auditorium which would seat hundreds to smaller rooms for twenty persons and up. According to Maddigan, the science fiction fans had the main auditorium for the next four days.

I crossed the street and entered the foyer. A directory, right opposite the entrance, listed those events scheduled for the day.

Assembly Hall: Socialist Labor Party; speaker, Damon Long; subject: "Capitalism Means War." 8 P.M.

South Hall: Church of the Advent; speaker, Reverend Joseph David; subject: "Has Jesus Already Returned?" 7:30 P.M.

"Washington Hall: United Vegetarians; speaker, Claude Moro-
witz; subject: "Is Mankind Omnivorous?" 8 P.M.

Auditorium: World Science Fiction Convention. Noon.

I looked around to spot someone who could tell me where the
auditorium was. It wasn't necessary. In the door came a grown
man dressed like Flash Gordon, with a transparent plastic helmet
over his head and a child's rocket pistol at his belt.

"Oh, *no,*" I groaned inaudibly.

Flash Gordon turned to the right and ascended the staircase
there. I followed him. If he didn't belong to the science fiction
convention, then I didn't belong to the human race.

There they were, all right. The auditorium's entrance was on
the second floor of the Sherman Halls. The doors opened on the
back of the hall, which slanted forward gently to a comfortable-
sized stage. Even from the entrance, I could see that the local
members had gone to considerable trouble decorating the place for
their convention. I shuddered.

Flash Gordon marched on inside and I began to follow, but a
bright young thing in sweater, skirt and bobby sox, sitting at a
desk at the door, asked smilingly, "Have you registered yet?"

I looked down at her. "No. Where do I register?" She said,
"Here," looking as though I wasn't very bright. "That will be one
dollar."

"All right," I told her. I paid the dollar, signed a book, gave her
my name and address and watched as she typed up that vital information on a registration card. The registration card I put in a
pocket; the pin she gave me went on my coat. I was now evidently
eligible to enter.

First she said, "Are you acquainted? Would you like one of the
local fans to take you around? I don't believe I've seen you before—"

"I'll make out," I told her. "Is Ross Maddigan about?"

"He was here a minute ago. Ross is on the committee."

"How about Les Zimmer or Art Roget?"

"Well, Les is supposed to be ill at home, but I imagine he'll be
down later anyway." She smiled, as though we had a secret between us. "You know Les; he couldn't be kept away by a spaceship full of Aldeberans."

I shot her a quick glance, but she hadn't meant anything by it;
evidently what had happened to Les Zimmer hadn't made the
rounds as yet. I felt like telling her, "That's what you think," but I
kept it to myself.

She said, "I think I saw Art around a few minutes ago. Are you a pro?" She arched an eyebrow.

I blinked at her. "Come again?"

"You aren't a professional—a writer, or editor, or maybe an illustrator?" She was shaking her head slightly as though she already knew the answer.

"Oh. I thought you meant something else. No. No, I'm not."

She moved a shoulder and said sadly, "I didn't think you were."

Not knowing how to take that, I let it go and entered the auditorium.

There must have been a good two hundred persons present at that stage, about one quarter of them female. Possibly twenty-five or thirty were in costume. And when I say costume, I mean exactly that. My Flash Gordon pal was conservative. Half a dozen I could more or less make out—no more. A red devil, complete with trident and tail and horns; an Arabian Djinn with a scimitar as long as his leg; a vampire with a long black cloak and a white face well equipped with fangs. The others were more intricate. There was, for instance, what probably was meant to be a spider-man from Saturn, or some such; a child must have been in that costume, since the spider-man was only about four and a half feet tall.

Next to me was standing a man with one of the transparent plastic raincoats the women are wearing currently over his head. Through the top of the raincoat were sticking half a dozen tremendous darning needles. I tried to figure it out, watching him from the side of my eyes, but it wouldn't come.

Finally, I indicated the get-up and said, "Buddy, what goes on?"

He said, "The masquerade starts tonight and some of us are already in costume."

I couldn't stand it any longer. I said, "What are you supposed to be?"

He stared at me, combining haughtiness and contempt for my ignorance. "I'm a pre-natal engram."

"Come again?"

"A pre-natal engram. Haven't you read dianetics?"

"I haven't even heard of it."

He snorted disgustedly, said, "You didn't *look* clear to me," and stalked away.

I looked about the hall. Along the sides were erected a score or so of tables loaded with books and magazines. Some had signs advertising this or that publishing house. I only recognized one or two of the names. I found out later that the science-fantasy field has a half-dozen or more small publishers of its own.

I began to stalk around easily, wondering what it was that Roget and Maddigan thought I might be able to find here. The books on the table were stacked in neat piles; most of them had covers on the loudish side. They seemed to be fairly well done otherwise.

I stopped at one table on which there were at least twenty-five different publications and picked up one of them at random. *Without Sorcery,* by Theodore Sturgeon. It was a collection of shorts which had evidently been reprinted from original magazine stories.

A youngster next to me gushed, "Don't you think Sturgeon is wonderful?"

"Uh?" I grunted at him. Then, "Oh, oh sure. He's out of this world." I put the book down and went on to the next exhibit. This table was loaded with old magazines, scores of them. The owner was busily arguing with half a dozen potential customers at once. I picked up one of the publications and thumbed through it. It was pretty well worn, the date was 1939, the cover was gruesome, and the title of the magazine was *Unknown.*

The table's proprietor said, "Trying to complete your collection?"

"Not exactly," I told him. Something else seemed to be in order, so I asked, "What's the price on this?" reaching in my pocket for some change. I figured that I'd look more authentic wandering around the hall if I was carrying a magazine with me.

"Three dollars," he told me.

I glared at him indignantly. "You batty? This magazine is falling apart; it's more than ten years old."

He took it from my hand with as little gentleness as was consistent with the magazine's condition, and glared back. "That's the issue in which *Sinister Barrier* was first—"

"All right, all right," I cut him off, "keep it." I got on to the next table before he assaulted me.

It was piled principally with anthologies. *Big Book of Science Fiction,* edited by Groff Conklin, *The Best Science Fiction Stories of 1950,* edited by Bleiler and Dikty, *Men Against the Stars, Adventures in Time and Space, My Best Science Fiction Story.* There must have been at least twenty of them. I thumbed through two or three. A dozen or so authors seemed to predominate: Ray

Bradbury, A. E. Van Vogt, Robert Heinlein, Henry Kuttner, Fredric Brown, Eric Frank Russell, Cleve Cartmill.

I had begun to skim through a story entitled *Rat Race* by John and Dorothy de Courcy when a voice said, "Hello, Knight. Finding anything of interest?" I looked up at Art Roget. He had his Jimmy Stewart grin back again.

I put the book back and we shook hands. "Just looking around, getting the lay of the land," I told him.

He said, "What did you think of the Zimmer affair?" We moved over to one side, out of earshot of the milling fans.

"I don't know," I said impatiently. "I don't get it. Did you read that report I sent you and Maddigan?"

He nodded and remained silent as though he expected me to say something. I said, "That's all I know. I put it all in the report."

"Do you think the extra-terrestrials actually fired a heat ray at Les?" He sounded eager, as though hoping I'd say yes.

I disappointed him. "No, I don't," I said.

"Well, what *do* you think? What conclusion did you come to?"

I stared out over the convention hall. I didn't have an answer for him—not really. I said, "I haven't come to a conclusion. I don't know enough about what's going on." I paused a minute, then asked, "Listen, did you subscribe to Harry Shulman's little magazine?"

Roget shook his head and began to say something, but I cut him off.

"How come?" I protested. "You belonged to the same club, you used to issue one together—"

He explained, "There're probably fifty or more fanzines being published in the United States alone, not to speak of Canada, England, Australia, and a few odds and ends of other countries. I take about ten of these. I can't afford any more. I didn't particularly like *Off-Trail Fantasy;* Harry was always getting worked up about this, that, or the other thing. At any rate, I didn't subscribe. I get McCain's *Wastebasket,* Don Day's *Fan-scient,* and . . ."

"All right. You didn't happen, just by chance, to see a copy of the current *Off-Trail Fantasy?* Possibly someone else had one . . ."

"No, I don't think it's out yet."

I said absently, "He had the new issue stashed away in his cellar ready for mailing. Somebody stole them all, burgled the house since his death."

"What!" he ejaculated. If I'd suddenly grown antlers, he couldn't have looked more surprised.

"That's right," I said. "Possibly tied up in that magazine is the motive—the real motive for Harry's death."

His mouth was sagging; he snapped it shut and shook his head. "I don't know," he said. "I don't know at all. Knight, when Maddigan first suggested hiring you, I thought the whole idea ridiculous. It's all right making a hobby of investigating the possibility of alien life, but to take it that seriously—"

"That's what Ross Maddigan said," I muttered.

"Well, that's how I felt at first. It was just ridiculous that James Maddigan should spend his good money hiring a detective."

"All right," I said, "but now?"

Art Roget rubbed his chin, as though checking on his morning shave. "Now I don't know, Knight. It just piles up too much. I've been thinking it over, and over and over again, and the only thing that makes sense is that there *are* extra-terrestrials here on earth, anxious to keep us in the dark about their activities."

We stood there another ten minutes, silent most of the time, both of us thinking. Abstractedly, Roget pointed out a half-dozen of the science fiction celebrities about the hall; abstractedly, I listened to what he said.

Finally, "Somebody said Bob Carr was here; maybe we ought to talk to him," Roget said.

"Who's Bob Carr?"

"Haven't met him myself, but he's a fan who's really hepped on the possibility of alien life forms; he's done a lot of articles about it."

"Oh, yeah," I said. "I think Ross mentioned him. Doesn't he come from the Middle West somewhere?"

"Ummm," he answered, looking out over the crowd. "I think Ross knows him; if we could locate Ross he could introduce us. It might be a good idea to go to one of the rooms and bat the breeze with him for a while."

I looked around for Ross Maddigan too. He didn't seem to be present, unless, of course, he was under one of the costumes. Off hand, Ross didn't appear to me a guy who'd get himself up in costume, at least not this early in the day.

But I spotted somebody I *did* want to see. I said to Roget, "Listen, suppose you try and scout him out. I'll wander around here looking for him."

"Okay," he said, "there isn't any particular hurry." He wedged himself into the crowd and was off.

I set off in another direction, making my way toward Julie Sharp who stood, cool and amused, at the entrance to the hall.

She was wearing a dark-blue sheer wool dress which went far to remind you of her figure, but which, by its very simplicity, denied it was doing it. There were pearls at her throat and one at each lobe of her ears. The dab of blue cloth on the edge of her head was a hat.

"Hello," I told her, "thought you weren't enough of a fan to wind up here."

She arched her eyebrow at me, behind her king-size, swash-shaped glasses. "And how about you?" Her voice was as softly throaty as I'd remembered it.

I grinned at her. "I'm working."

I led her to one side, where we could hear ourselves think. She said, "I have the afternoon off, so I thought I'd drop in for an hour or so. Ross said these conventions are a lot of fun. Which reminds me, have you seen him?"

I shook my head. "I was trying to find Ross myself."

She said idly, but with an imp peering from within velvet-blue eyes, "Found any little green men yet?"

I said, "How did you know I was looking for little green men? Besides, everybody tells me they aren't necessarily green."

She laughed under her breath. "Ross told me. What color are they?"

I played it serious. "Nobody knows; purple maybe."

"You ought to be ashamed, taking money for such a job."

"Don't I know it?" I growled. "Trouble is, I need the dough too badly to have scruples. How far can a guy sink, Julie?"

She finished her search of the hall. "I recognize a few of them here, but I don't see Ross. Possibly he's down at the bar."

"The bar?"

Julie turned her eyes back to me. "These conventions, so Ross tells me, are just one long binge—at least for a good many of the attenders. Especially the professionals, I suspect."

"But they don't have a bar in here."

She said, "There's one next door at the Bigelow. Most of the fans have taken rooms there; that is, the ones from out of town. In fact, I believe Ross has a room too, just so he'll be handy for the four days of the convention—save him from going back and forth from home."

"All right, let's go." I took her by the arm and led her toward the door. Her flesh, warm beneath my hand, was softly feminine—

the warmth spread through my body and I felt my mouth go dry. This girl really had it —and in very large quantities.

As we walked down the steps, we passed the little spider-man I'd noticed earlier and Julie said, "Heavens, what a cute little fellow."

He looked back over his shoulder and leered. "You ain't so bad yourself, baby." Our spider-man was only four and a half feet tall, but his voice was that of a grown man. He added, "How you comin', Jeb?"

It was Tiny! He'd gone on before I got over my surprise.

Julie looked after him and laughed. "He seemed to know you," she said questioningly.

"My newsdealer," I told her. "I didn't recognize him at first. He used to be with a carnival." I brought the subject back to a point we'd let drop. "Why should the professionals go in for more liquid refreshment than the others?"

We were passing jabbering groups of fans as we progressed toward the Bigelow and its oasis. Most of them were arguing heatedly. I was beginning to get used to the fact that the fen took their science fiction seriously.

Julie Sharp didn't really know. "But I've got a sneaking suspicion that on the average the fans are a good deal more earnest about this than the professionals. For the fan, it's the big thing in life, deadly earnest; for the pro, it's a living, and most people are able to get rather philosophical about their manner of making a living."

We reached the lobby, went out into the street, and headed along the sidewalk toward the Bigelow. There was a street entrance to the cocktail lounge, and we saved ourselves a trip through the hotel foyer.

The lounge was well filled, all the tables being taken, but we found two stools. Among the bartender's patrons were two or three costumed fans. At the tables, the arguments were going on heatedly about science fiction versus fantasy; writer Van Vogt versus writer Heinlein; illustrator Hannes Bok versus illustrator Cartier; *Astounding* versus *Planet.* The lone bartender needed help; he was dashing around with all the verve of a whirling dervish in a revolving door, but he was losing out. It wasn't just a matter of beer and straight shots with an occasional Tom Collins order. They wanted a John Brown's Body, a couple of Zombies and half a dozen other of the more intricate concoctions. One costumed fan, already well into his cups, was loudly demanding a Martian *woji.*

I looked at Julie, who was laughing at it all. "Let's make it simple for him," I suggested.

"This weather calls for beer, anyway," she agreed.

I told the harassed bartender, "Two beers, please."

He said from the heart, "Thanks, folks," as he popped the tops off the bottles of Bud. He added wistfully, "I been in the business twenty years, but what the hell's a John Brown's Body?—Pardon my language, miss."

Julie told him seriously, "I don't blame you."

I dropped a dollar bill onto the bar, but he was too harried to make change. He dashed off to take more orders, and to pull a shaker of frozen daiquiris from his mixer.

Julie sipped her beer and said, "He must feel like he's in a den of Bems."

"Den of what?"

She said, "You know, Jeb, that's how I first spotted you at Ross's party as not really being a fan. You didn't know what a Bem was."

"All right, so you spotted me. I still don't know."

"A bug-eyed monster."

I took a swallow of the beer and looked back at her. "I don't think I got that."

She laughed, that light laugh of hers. "Jeb, I think your greatest charm is that you usually don't quite get it. Well, anyway, in science fiction stories when the writers are trying to describe an alien life form, they almost invariably dream up some horrible-looking creature which the fans dub Bems, bug-eyed monsters."

"All right," I conceded, "I don't know how we got side-tracked like this. Didn't we come looking for Ross?"

"Ross isn't here," she said; then the imp was in her eyes again. "Do you really want to find him?"

I ran my eyes about the place as though just noting the fact. "You're right," I told her; "let's have another drink and figure out what we ought to do about it." I motioned to the bartender and made circular motions with my hand over our glasses. He nodded and in another couple of minutes had fresh ones before us.

"Jeb," Julie said, "some nice girl ought to take you in hand."

"I'm available," I told her eagerly.

Just then a bellhop stuck his head in the door and called, "Mr. Knight. Paging Mr. Knight. Mr. Knight."

CHAPTER FOURTEEN

I SWORE INWARDLY, but looked over at the bellboy and called, "That's me."

The bellboy was no boy; he was at least thirty and his bored cynicism, acquired over the years, had begun to bring out highlights of sophistication, craftiness and misanthropy in his face. He came closer to be handy for a tip and said, "Phone call, Mr. Knight."

"All right," I said. I turned back to Julie. "Would you mind waiting here? Only be a minute."

She smiled. "Not at all."

I followed the bellhop to the lobby and he indicated the house phones which were sheltered in a small alcove to one side of the reservation desk. "You can take it here," he said. I slipped him a dime. He scowled at it, pocketed it, and left without thanks. What was he expecting—did I look like a movie star?

I took up one of the half-dozen phones and said, "This is Jeb Knight; there was a call for me."

The operator whined, "Just a moment, please."

A new voice said, "Good afternoon; Maddigan and Maddigan." There was the sound of typewriters in the background, and the voice was that of one of James Maddigan's office girls. I remembered her tone.

"This is Jeb Knight," I told her.

"One moment, please, I'll connect you with Mr. Maddigan." There was another click and Maddigan's worried voice said, "Knight?"

"Speaking, Mr. Maddigan. What can I do for you?"

"How's the convention going?"

"All right, I guess," I told him. "This is my first, so I can hardly compare them."

"I'll be through here at the office in possibly two hours and shall come down immediately. Are there many in attendance?"

"Couple of hundred or so, I'd say." I wondered if he'd called me to find out how the convention was being attended, to check on whether I was really here earning my dough, or what.

He said, "Knight, I thought of something after I conversed with you last. You'll recall you wished to know whether or not I subscribed to Harry Shulman's fanzine?"

"Yes."

"It has just occurred to me that Ross does. My nephew Ross. Possibly he has a copy of the current issue."

"I doubt it," I said thoughtfully. "It looks as though the whole edition was there in Harry's cellar except, of course, for the single copy he gave me."

"Oh, did he give you a copy? You hadn't mentioned it in your reports, Knight."

"I would have in the one I did up tonight. Anyway, it's been stolen from my office desk. I never had a chance to read it."

"Amazing," he said; then, hesitantly, "Well, I merely called you to inform you that Ross received Shulman's fanzine and that he reserved accommodations there at the hotel; if you are unable to find him elsewhere, I suggest that you try his room."

I told him I'd get right to it, and hung up.

I went back to the bar, but Julie Sharp's stool was empty. I got back on mine and ordered another beer. She didn't return, so I finished off my drink and gave it up.

I went back into the lobby and up to the desk clerk to ask what room Ross Maddigan was in. The clerk was an impeccably dressed young man with a thin mustache and with thin eyebrows. He reminded me of Mr. Whipple in the Tilly the Toiler cartoon strip. He checked and told me Ross Maddigan was in 1104 and that since his key wasn't in the box he must be up there.

As I turned to look for the elevators, a fan, dressed in the God-awfulest costume of the convention, sauntered up the desk behind me and tossed a key to the blotter before the clerk. His costume and mask were purple and he had an extra pair of limbs jutting from his sides beneath his regular arms. He carried a small suitcase in one hand, undoubtedly full of magazines and books for trading up in the auditorium.

I shook my head and muttered, "They aren't necessarily green." I went over to the elevators and waited for a car. Three or four of the fen crowded in with me when it came, their arms full of suspiciously tinkling packages. I told myself I was glad I wasn't the house dick in charge here tonight.

The fans clambered out at the tenth floor, and the elevator girl closed the door behind them and leaned against the wall momentarily. "Whooo," she sighed. "And yesterday I thought I'd carried every kind of person in the country up and down this shaft."

"Live and learn," I told her. "Floor eleven, please."

She asked, "Did you see that one in the purple costume?"

"Yeah," I said. "A honey."

"I just brought him down," she said. "He told me he was a Martian." We reached the eleventh and she slid the door open expertly.

I said, "Maybe he was."

She looked at me suspiciously as I left.

Tiny golden arrows on the cream-colored walls indicated the directions of the room numbers. 1104 was to my right. As I searched it out, I ran into small groups of fans standing in the corridors squabbling in their science fiction patois. Sometimes an open door would reveal a half-dozen sitting around, glasses in hand, earnestly arguing about step-rockets, time machines, the H-bomb.

I went down one corridor, up another. The numbers were getting nearer to the one I was seeking: 1112, 1110, 1108, 1106. I turned a corner and stopped short to avoid stepping on the body sprawled there flat on its face.

Along the back of my neck the short hair stiffened. For a brief second, I thought it was Ross Maddigan. I bent down quickly and tried to turn it over; the body was limp and warm. On the chest the suit's cloth still smoldered. There was an ugly burn on the breast and a smell of ozone, burning flesh and cloth in the air.

I could hear voices approaching from behind me. One said, "Bradbury's deserted us; he's gone over to the slicks. The trouble is that—"

A trio of gasps and grunts followed that, and I looked up over my shoulder at them. I snapped, "Call the house detective, real quick. And after that tell the desk there's been a serious accident up here."

One of them, staring down at the body with wide-eyed fascination, blurted, "It's Bob Carr. He's been hurt."

Something suddenly occurred to me. I snapped, "Listen, does one of you have the correct time?" It was to turn out to be the smartest thing I'd done all week.

In seconds, the three of them had disappeared. While I waited for the house dick, I tried the door of 1104; it was locked. I knocked without result. Maybe Ross Maddigan had his key, but he wasn't in his room.

I dug my pipe out of my side pocket, automatically loaded and lighted it, staring down at the body of young Carr.

He was another kid, possibly even a bit younger than either Shulman or Zimmer; probably not out of his teens. According to what they'd all said, he was the outstanding science fiction fan authority on extra-terrestrial life, and the possibility that it had already discovered how to journey to earth.

Carr didn't look as though he'd ever been an authority about anything. His body was that of a rag doll's; his eyes were still expressing horror and shock, and the scar on his chest was ugly blue, green and red. It wasn't a bullet hole. I didn't know what it was.

The house dick rumbled up excitedly, a thick, semi-bald, big-bellied customer who could easily have weighed two hundred and forty pounds. He shot a quick glance from me down to the corpse and up again. "What's the matter with him?" he rapped.

"He's dead," I said. "I found him. A couple of these science fiction fans were here a minute ago; one of them said his name was Bob Carr. That's all I can tell you."

He bent down over the body and inspected the ugly chest wound. His head came up and he stared up and down the corridor. "This is crazy," he said. "This guy looks like he's been electrocuted."

I told him, "You'd better get in touch with Lieutenant Davis at Homicide. He's on the case."

He scowled at me. "What d'ya mean, 'he's on the case'?"

I made an impatient gesture. "This is the third one. At least the second. Only one of the other two attempts was successful."

"You mean there's been more of these?" he asked unbelievingly. "Who's been doing it?"

Here we went again. "The best we can do so far is to say, probably some men from Mars," I told him sourly.

He closed his eyes, then opened them. He said, "Who in hell are *you*, Jack?" There was a wary inflection.

"Private investigator," I said. "I've been working on it too."

He said, "You better stay right here. I already phoned the cops."

I didn't answer him. What did he think I was going to do, try and make a desperate getaway?

His eyes went up and down the corridor. "How could a guy get electrocuted here?" he complained. "It just ain't possible. Brother, the management is going to love this. A guest gets electrocuted in the Bigelow just walking down the hall."

I went tut-tut-tut with my tongue as though I sympathized deeply with him, and he shot me another suspicious glance.

Arthur Roget rounded the corner suddenly, as though he'd been half running. He skidded to a stop and stared down at the crumpled body. "It's Bob Carr," he blurted.

I said interestedly, "I thought you didn't know Carr."

His eyes came up to mine. "How was he killed? Down below, the rumor is going all around that his chest looks almost completely burned out."

The house dick rapped, "Who are you?"

Roget's eyes went from him to me and back, then did a repeat.

I said, "He's one of the science fiction crowd. Part of the convention."

Ross Maddigan rounded the corner in much the same manner Roget had. "What's going on—" he began; then his eyes widened and went down to the body. "Good Lord, what's happened?" He was breathing excitedly.

"He's dead," I told him, "probably electrocuted. There's a burn on his chest that seems to be the point where he was—"

Art Roget said, awe in his voice, "It must have been some kind of ray gun."

The house dick looked from one to the other of us "You all sound like you're nuts," he said bitterly. "What d'ya know about this?" he demanded of Ross Maddigan.

Ross shook his head silently, staring down at the body as though fascinated.

"It's right in front of your room," I told him softly.

He stared up at the numbered door. "That's true," he said, as though just realizing it. His eyes went up and down the hallway. "There isn't any way he could have been electrocuted in this corridor," he said unbelievingly.

Art Roget blabbered, "It was some kind of ray gun, I tell you. Maybe the same thing they fired at Les Zimmer."

"Who's *they?*" the house dick rapped at him.

"The extra-terrestrials," Roget said, his eyes reflecting fear, almost terror. "Maybe from Mars or Venus; maybe—"

The detective snorted disgustedly. "You all three screwy?"

I said to Ross, "Did you see Julie?"

He nodded his head, his eyes still on Carr in shocked fascination. "A few minutes ago. She said you were looking for me."

"If you don't mind saying, where've you been the last half-hour?"

He shook his head, still dazedly. "Just wandering around; watching how things are going. I'm on the committee."

My pipe had gone out. I lit it again and scowled worriedly at him. "You'd better work out a more complete story than that, Ross. Davis'll be here in a matter of minutes, and here Carr's body is, right in front of your door. Don't forget that Harry Shulman's body was discovered in your garden. Davis is getting desperate enough to—"

A voice behind me said, "Davis is getting desperate enough to do what, eh?" The voice was soft but not pleasant.

I turned and said, under my breath, "Oh, *no.*" Then out loud, "Hello, Lieutenant. I was just telling Maddigan here that you'd probably want an accounting of his time."

Davis's eyes didn't leave my face. "And yours, friend—and yours." He stared at me unblinkingly. Behind him, Sergeant Mike Quinn winked. "Martians again, Buster?" he asked.

Davis growled, without turning, "Shut up, Mike." He looked down at Bob Carr's body. "Who's this, eh?"

The house dick, Ross Maddigan and Art Roget started talking at once.

Davis said, "Hold it." He looked at Ross. "You're Ross Maddigan; that other killing took place over at your house?" Ross nodded and Davis's eyes went to Art Roget. "And you're one of the three that hired this half-baked private detective to investigate little green men?"

Art Roget began to say something protestingly, and Davis snapped, "I know; maybe they're purple." Roget looked as though he was going to protest that that wasn't what he was about to say, but Davis's flat eyes went to the house dick. "You're connected with the hotel?"

At the other's nod, he growled, "Any of these rooms available for us to work in?"

Ross Maddigan said hurriedly, "This is my room here, Lieutenant. You can work in there."

Mike Quinn said humorously, "You ain't kidding, we'll work in there."

Davis shot him an impatient look, then indicated the body with a thumb. "Anybody know what's happened to this man?"

The house dick said, "Looks like electrocution to me, Lieutenant. Listen, the management—"

Davis stared him down. "The devil with the management," he growled softly. His eyes went to Maddigan. "Open the door, eh?"

Ross Maddigan's hand went to his pocket. He said, "Sorry, I haven't got my key. It's at the desk. I could go down—"

The house dick said, "I've got a master key." He went to the door and opened it. Mike Quinn made his way to the phone, which stood on a small table next to the bed, picked it up carefully, fingerprint conscious, and phoned headquarters. The police machine was beginning to roll.

I shot a quick look into the bathroom, particularly up at the light socket above the lavatory. Nothing seemed unusually out of the way.

Davis said to me disgustedly, *"We'll* investigate all the possibilities of his being killed in this room with the house current, Knight. You can just stop worrying about it. Sit down. Mike, get out at the end of that corridor and keep any of those blasted crackpots from getting in here, eh?"

Mike Quinn left the room, and Davis sank down on the edge of the bed and ran his eyes over us wearily.

"Okay, you three, let's have it. What happened?" He sneered nastily, then, "Or at least what do you *say* happened?"

I said, "I found Carr, Lieutenant."

"How did you know his name—" he began to snap.

"Some fans who knew him came along a minute after me," I said. Then: "I came up here looking for Ross Maddigan."

"Why?"

"I wanted to find out whether or not he had a copy of the last issue of *Off-Trail Fantasy,* Harry Shulman's fan magazine."

Ross Maddigan said, "It isn't out yet."

Lieutenant Davis showed no signs of having heard him; his eyes were on me, gray, washed out. He said, very slowly and very softly, "Why did you want a copy of Shulman's magazine, Knight?"

I took a deep breath. "I'd heard they'd all disappeared and I thought maybe there was something in—"

"Okay, Knight," he interrupted, still softly, "so you came looking for Maddigan. Then what?" He looked searchingly at his left thumb.

I let my shoulder rise and fall. "I found him, Bob Carr, lying there in the hall. His coat was still smoking and I could smell, well, kind of an ozone smell in the air."

"So you found the body, eh?" He nodded, almost as though in satisfaction. "Okay, and then?"

"Like I said, some fans rounded the corner and saw him and one said it was Bob Carr. I sent them to call the house detective."

"Why not a doctor, eh?"

"I could see he was already dead. I turned him over first."

"Dammit, Knight, don't you even know you shouldn't touch a body until the medical examiner arrives?"

"I didn't know it was a body until after I touched it," I told him.

Mike Quinn stuck his head in the doorway. "The boys are beginning to arrive, Phil."

Davis didn't look away from me. He growled from the side of his mouth, "Let me know as soon as possible what that stiff died from, eh?" Mike Quinn said okay and his head disappeared again.

Quinn came to his feet and headed for the bathroom, reaching his right thumb and forefinger into his vest pocket to emerge with a small bottle. The rest of us sat quietly while water ran; then he returned to the door, glass in hand. He tossed two pills into his mouth and washed them down.

Another head made itself evident at the door, a patrolman's. He said, "Lieutenant, you got a guy named Roget here, Arthur Roget?"

Art Roget cleared his throat and said nervously, "That's my name, Officer."

The patrolman looked him over, then turned back to Davis. "Lieutenant, we gotta fella down there says this Arthur Roget has been looking for this guy Carr for the past hour or so."

"Thanks, Bill," Davis said. His eyes went to Art Roget. "What'd you want Carr for, eh?"

Roget's face was pale now. His tongue came out and licked over his lips. He said, fear in his voice, "Jeb Knight and I were both looking for him."

"My pal," I muttered, under my breath.

Lieutenant Davis's pale eyes went over me again. He went back to Roget and said smoothly, "Why? Why were you and Knight looking for Carr, eh?"

Roget's eyes went pleadingly to me. Mike Quinn reentered the room, evidently with more news on the progress of the boys working out in the corridor.

I said, "This Bob Carr was an authority on alien life forms. We wanted to ask him what he thought about the possibility of there being extra-terrestrials on earth."

"Oh, brother," Mike Quinn laughed. "Buster's at it again."

CHAPTER FIFTEEN

IT WAS ANOTHER three hours or more before I got out of there.

Davis began by concentrating on me. We had the bartender up and Julie Sharp; we had the bellhop, the phone operator, the desk clerk and the elevator girl. We had the three fans who had come up right behind me as I discovered Carr's body; and in particular, the one that I'd remembered to ask the time.

They all recalled me well enough, but only the desk clerk was able to be of any real use as an alibi. He'd known the approximate time I'd asked him Ross's room number; he'd just got back to the desk after a late lunch. It was less than ten minutes after I'd talked to him that the fan in the corridor had looked at his watch.

Davis finally gave up on that angle. He growled at me, "It wouldn't have been impossible for you to have got up here and chilled this Bob Carr in the time you had—but I'll admit it wouldn't have been very probable."

He sat in thought for a long moment. Ross Maddigan and Art Roget were still in the room with us; the house dick had gone to report to the management. I didn't envy him. Maddigan, Roget and I waited quietly—quakingly might be the better term.

Davis said finally, "This guy James Maddigan, where does he come in?"

I told him once more. "He and Arthur Roget, here, are my clients. This was to be the last day I worked on the case. They wanted me to take in the convention, on the theory that if there were any extra-terrestrials in this city they'd come to a science fiction convention just to check on whether or not we humans were getting wise to them."

Mike Quinn snickered.

I went on. "I didn't say it made sense; I'm just telling you what Maddigan and Roget wanted me to do. All right, I'd told James Maddigan about Harry Shulman's magazines disappearing. I thought perhaps he was a subscriber and might have received one before Shulman's death. He wasn't a subscriber; not that it would have made any difference, because evidently Shulman hadn't got any copies out into the mail. But while I was in the bar talking to

Miss Sharp, Maddigan remembered that his nephew, Ross, was a subscriber. He phoned the hotel, had me paged, and told me about it, suggesting that I look Ross up."

"Where'd he call from?" Davis asked thoughtfully.

"From his office. He had some last minute work to clear up, then he was going to come down here."

"How do you know he was in his office when he called?"

"I talked to his office girl first; besides, I could hear the typewriters going in the background. What's your point?"

He shot me a glare. "I'll ask the questions, Knight. You just answer them, eh? Did you know this guy Carr?"

"I already told you I didn't," I said irritably. We weren't getting anywhere; Davis was beginning to rehash the whole thing, beginning to end. "He comes from somewhere in the Middle West, Indianapolis, I think. I'd never heard about him until Ross mentioned Carr's interest in alien life forms."

Davis turned to Mike Quinn. "Get this Les Zimmer guy over here, Mike. And keep trying to locate this guy James Maddigan, eh? Where is he, anyway?"

Mike Quinn said, "He's supposed to be on his way, according to his secretary. He left about a half-hour after the killing; his office is on Oglethorpe and West First Street, so he oughta be here any minute."

"Okay, bring him in as soon as he shows," Davis turned to Art Roget. "Did you know this Bob Carr?"

Roget shook his head emphatically. "No sir, I told you that before. I'd read some of his things in the fanzines, but I'd never met him. This was the first time he ever came to this city as far as I know. I don't think anybody among the local fen had met him except Ross."

Davis's eyes went to Ross. "Well?"

Ross Maddigan's good-natured face was frowning earnestly. He said, "I was passing through Indianapolis on my way West about two years ago. I had a correspondent there and phoned him; he said the local science fiction club was to meet that night and wanted me to attend, so I did. I met Bob Carr at that meeting, along with a dozen others of the Indiana fen. That's the only contact I've ever had with him."

Davis took time out to reach into his vest pocket for his pills again. He had set the half consumed glass of water on the desk next to him; now he shook out one pill and swallowed it down with a sigh.

"You haven't even corresponded with him since, eh?"

Ross shook his head. "No. I'm not sure I would have recognized him, we met so briefly."

The lieutenant breathed deeply, weariness making his pallor even more pronounced. He said to Ross. "Then what do you think he was doing outside your door?"

"How should I know? Possibly he came up looking for me. After all, I was the only person in town he knew even the slightest bit."

"Then, as far as you know, there is nobody in this city that even knew Carr, let alone had a reason for killing him, eh?"

"That's right. Of course, some of the other Indiana fen are in town for the convention. They knew—"

Davis brushed that aside. "This was done by a local boy, not somebody that just pulled in from Indiana yesterday or today. This is part of the other two—"

Art Roget blurted, "It's just like Harry and Les. The same thing. There isn't any motive; not any human one. The only reason anything would want to kill Harry, or Les, or Bob was because they were fen who—"

"Knock it off," Davis growled. "The police department doesn't go chasing men from Mars."

"I'm beginning to think that perhaps you should," Ross Maddigan said so softly that he could hardly be heard. He stared down at the toe of his brown sport shoe. "I thought Uncle Jim was being fantastic, hiring Jeb Knight to investigate alien life forms—now I don't know."

Davis snorted and turned his empty eyes back to me. "Where'd you find out that Shulman's magazines were missing, eh?"

I thought quickly and came up with an answer that was near enough to the truth but would still protect Hermie Cain. "Mrs. Shulman told me."

He said carefully, "Actually, Knight, I oughta run you in. I'd feel better about this case if you were in the cooler."

"Listen, for crying out loud," I complained, "on what charge?"

"You're a material witness, Knight. And I'm not too sure you don't know more about this than you're telling." He added, irrelevantly, I thought, "I hate a wise guy cluttering up my work."

I started to say something, but he rapped, "Shut up and get out of here before I change my mind."

I got to my feet, preparatory to leaving.

"And listen, Knight. You haven't got a client any more, not after today. So if I have any more trouble with you on this case, I'll make you rue it. Understand?"

"As you said, Lieutenant, I haven't a client any more."

As I left, I met Mike Quinn ushering Julie Sharp up the hall. Evidently Davis wanted to speak to her again—when I wasn't present.

Quinn said, "You leaving so soon, Buster?"

I ignored the pop-eyed clown and said to Julie, "Sorry this is all happening; we were just getting acquainted, there at the bar."

Her eyes smiled at me. "Heavens, there'll be other times, Jeb."

They passed on and I looked after them. Did I say *them?* I meant *her.* I've mentioned her legs, haven't I?

The same elevator girl was on duty. I entered the car and said, "Lobby, please."

On the main floor, I went over to the desk. I said to the clerk I'd talked to before, "Thanks, buddy; you were more help than you can imagine."

He said stiffly, "I simply told the truth."

"Sure, and thanks. But listen. Remember, I asked you Ross Maddigan's room number and you told me, and then said his key wasn't in its box?"

He frowned, his thin, neat eyebrows coming almost together. I owed him my neck, probably, but I still thought he looked like Mr. Whipple in Tillie the Toiler. He said, "I'd forgotten that about the key. I remember you asking for his room number." He looked back at the box. "The key's there now."

I felt a cold finger trace lightly up my back.

"You sure?" I looked over his shoulder. There was a key in box 1104, all right.

It stopped me. While I stood there, trying to make sense out of something that didn't fit together, he went off to wait on someone. I didn't move away, so when he was through he came back again.

He said, "Was there something else?"

"Do you know Ross Maddigan?" I said slowly. "That is, by sight?"

He shook his head. "It would hardly be possible, considering the fantastic costume he's wearing."

He must have noticed my expression because he added, "Mr. Maddigan is wearing a costume today." He sniffed superciliously, and the tiny mustache twitched. "I assume he represents a Martian or something."

Involuntarily, I put my hand out and grasped his wrist. "Listen, did you give Ross Maddigan's key to someone in a costume?"

"What do you mean, *some one in a costume?*" he said indignantly, drawing his arm from under my hand. "When Mr. Maddigan asked for his key, I gave it to him. It was none of my business if he was in costume."

"How did you know it was Ross Maddigan?"

He stared at me. "Why—why, he just—why, I don't know. He asked for his key and I gave it to him." He batted his eyes apprehensively.

"When was this?" I was still excited.

"I don't remember exactly; just before I went to lunch, I believe."

"When did he bring it back again? When I talked to you it was gone."

He was worried now. His thin eyebrows edged together. "I really don't know. So many guests just toss their keys to the desk, you know. We put them in their proper boxes when we get the time."

I snapped my fingers. "The fan in the purple costume, the one with the four arms and the suitcase. He tossed a key to the desk just as I finished talking to you."

"I didn't notice him, but that sounds like Mr. Maddigan's costume," he said doubtfully. "Perhaps I had better tell the police upstairs about this."

"Yeah," I told him, simmering down suddenly. "Yeah, I guess you'd better." I turned and headed for the cocktail lounge. It was none of my business, not any more, at least.

But I didn't stop at the bar. My business or not, this thing was too hot. I went out the public entrance of the bar and down the street a hundred feet or so to the entrance of the Sherman Halls. I took the steps up to the auditorium three at a time, excitement growing in me.

The bobby-soxer at the desk said, "Have you registered yet?" then spotted the pin on my lapel. "Oh, yes—" she finished inanely. I started to hurry on by her, but suddenly stopped and bent over the desk, my hands resting on its edge.

"Listen," I snapped, "did a fan come in here in a purple costume with four arms? He was carrying a small suitcase."

I could see now she was upset about something; probably the news of what had happened next door had spread. This convention wasn't going to be as much fun as a good many science fiction fans had expected. I wondered if they would continue it at all.

She shook her head, puzzled. "No. No, sir." Then: "Are you a detective; are you finding out about Bob?"

"No," I grunted over my shoulder. I hurried into the auditorium, just in case she'd made a mistake. There were less than half as many fans as there had been earlier. Most of those remaining didn't seem to be particularly interested in books and magazines, nor even in discussing science fantasy. They were still in little groups, but the air was full of murder, instead of rocket ships.

The four-armed and purple alien costume wasn't evident. I made doubly sure before turning around and leaving again. Of course he wouldn't have been there; I could have saved myself the excitement.

I went back to the Bigelow less hurriedly than I had left it. I walked into the lobby, still trying to make something of the fact that someone besides Ross Maddigan had got his key at the desk, and that a few minutes after he'd returned it, I stumbled upon a body in front of Ross' door.

I slumped down into a heavy lobby chair and tried to think. Actually, it didn't do much in the way of elimination. The person in the costume could have been male or female, short or tall, slim or heavy set.

Or it didn't necessarily *have* to be human.

I tossed my head impatiently at that. I was getting as bad as Art Roget.

As I sat there, staring before me, James Maddigan hustled into the lobby from the street. He showed indications that he had already heard about the Carr death. I came to my feet and he spotted me and hurried over.

"Good gracious, Knight, a fan outside just informed me that—"

I nodded. "It's another one along the same line as Shulman's death and the attack on Zimmer. Lieutenant Davis is upstairs; he wants to see you, Mr. Maddigan."

He nodded. "Yes, so I imagine, since it was my phone call that sent you up there." He took me by the arm. "Knight, I'd like a stimulant before facing that ordeal. Besides, I would like you to brief me on the situation. This is insane, absolutely, unbelievably insane. I don't—" His jowls were trembling.

He dragged me toward the bar, not that I needed much dragging.

We entered and found stools. The heavy buzz of conversation was still in the air, but it wasn't about Van Vogt and Kuttner, Hannes Bok and Cartier, any longer. As in the auditorium, it was about death—death by fantastic means.

I said to the bartender, "Beer." He had an assistant now and wasn't so harried.

Maddigan ordered, "Irish whiskey, please; double portion with water."

The bartender said to me, "They found out anything yet?"

I shook my head and began to answer him, but Maddigan snapped impatiently, in his most pompous tone, "Please, the drinks."

The bartender looked at him reproachfully and went off to get the order.

Maddigan turned to me and asked, "Just what occurred, Knight?"

I told him briefly while we waited for the drinks. When they came, Maddigan stiff-wristed his down and ordered another. I took a deep drink of my beer. We both seemed to need it.

"The killing must have taken place only minutes before I got there," I told him.

He frowned, his plump lips together in his peevish expression; he reached down and massaged his knee heavily. "Does that, of necessity, follow?"

I nodded. "I think so. For one thing, there were fans trooping up and down the corridors. They could hardly have failed to stumble on him in a very short time. And, besides, there was something else." I took another deep gulp.

Maddigan must have motioned to the bartender for still another drink, or possibly it was just that the bartender's intuition told him we were two customers who'd be wanting another round. At any rate, there was another bottle handy for me when I put the glass down, another double shot of Irish for Maddigan.

"What else?" Maddigan said.

"I saw the killer," I told him quietly.

His eyes bugged at me. "You what?"

"I saw the killer." I poured more beer into my glass from the fresh bottle and watched the head go down. "Just after talking to you, I went to the desk and asked for Ross's room. The clerk told me, and as I turned to leave, a costumed man—or woman, it could have been either—carrying a suitcase, tossed a key to the desk and left. Later on, just a few minutes ago, in fact, the clerk told me that he'd given Ross's key to a person in that get-up. In other words, somebody came to the desk, got Ross's key, and evidently did something in Ross's room that resulted in Carr's death."

"You mean you believe Bob Carr was killed in my nephew's room?"

"That's right," I nodded. "Killed there probably by use of the hotel's regular electric current, and then tossed out into the hall. That's the only answer that makes sense to me."

Half a dozen emotions chased themselves across James Maddigan's face. He was staring across the cocktail lounge, as though unbelieving of some of what I'd told him; as though seeing something he didn't want to believe.

He didn't say anything, so I said, "They're waiting upstairs, Mr. Maddigan, and already beginning to wonder what's keeping you. But before you go—I assume you won't need my services any longer?"

He brought his eyes back to me. "Eh? Oh." He thought a moment. "Yes, that is correct. As you pointed out the other day, as far as the investigation of the killing is concerned, the authorities are more efficient, more experienced." He paused. "Actually, I guess it was rather ridiculous of Art and me to consider that beings from space were committing those crimes."

He asked, "The police have still found no motive for any of the crimes?"

I shook my head. "This one is the worst of all. Nobody in our city has even been acquainted with Bob Carr, aside from Ross. There's just one possibility in my mind. That is, of course, barring that space aliens actually are at work."

"What possibility is that?"

"That some complete nut, somebody who's slipped his cogs but good, is behind it. Otherwise, it just doesn't make sense."

He was staring across the room again, but he brought his eyes back to me and said listlessly, "I imagine you're right." He held out a plump hand to be shaken. "At any rate, you've done what you could, Knight. You've neither proven nor disproven the presence of extra-terrestrials, but I'm convinced that it wasn't because of lack of effort on your part. In the future, if ever I have need of the services of a private investigator, I shall keep you in mind."

It was a nice little speech, even if not very accurate. Actually, I'd done damn little, if anything, to earn my money. However, I shook his hand and thanked him and he turned and left the bar, leaving me there to finish my beer.

I looked across the room to the point at which he'd been star-ing. Sandra Maddigan sat at a small corner table with a tall, well-dressed, good-looking guy of about thirty-five. Art Roget had ear-lier pointed him out to me up in the auditorium as Rog Craig, one of the most prolific of the science fiction writers. They had their heads together and evidently their conversation was interesting, for, they were ignoring their drinks.

CHAPTER SIXTEEN

IN THE MORNING, I stopped off at Tiny's for the papers. Brushing through the usual conglomeration of kids around the comic books, I picked up the three morning editions and worked my way back to where Tiny sat on his high stool behind the candy bars and cigarettes.

He laid his overgrown cigar on the edge of the counter and took the quarter I handed him. While he made change, I gave a quick glance at the headlines. The death of Harry Shulman hadn't made a particular stir—Carr's death did. The news rags had finally caught on. Two deaths, both by seemingly supernatural means, a science fiction convention background—all three papers, even the staid *Times,* were up in arms.

I looked up at Tiny.

His little face was expressionless. He took the cigar up again, put it in his mouth and said around it, "The *Chronicle* is particularly good. Got an editorial that wants you arrested for the murders. *Mirror's* got an editorial, too. They don't come right out and say it, but I think they wanta castrate you."

The newspapers weren't going to be enough reading material to tide me through the day. I turned away from Tiny and began edging myself along the racks looking for something interesting. Most of the magazines there I rejected by the appearance of their covers alone; some I picked up and thumbed through momentarily before putting them back.

Tiny said, "There's a new issue of *Super-Science Stories* just come out."

Without turning, I growled, "To hell with *Super-Science.* I've had enough science fiction to last me a lifetime."

I worked my way down past sport stories and love pulps, past air war magazines and adventure, past jungle stories and true detective. None of them looked particularly good to me and I finally wound up in front of the science-fantasy racks. Before I knew it, I'd picked up a copy of *Other Worlds* and was thumbing through it.

Tiny said, "There's a good story in that there mag by Fredric Brown."

"All right," I sighed. I turned back to him, tossed a quarter on the counter and put the digest size magazine in my pocket.

The big cigar was out of his mouth again and Tiny said casually, "That straight about you not working on this case any more?"

"Yeah, it's straight all right. I'm out of it, and well out of it."

"The newspapers said the Scylla Club hired you to investigate extra-terrestrials,"

"It was a gag at first," I told him patiently. "They were going to read my reports before the convention, just for laughs. I guess this new killing pretty well louses up the AnnConn."

"Yeah," he said, "and I was kind of looking forward to it for months. I don't think I'll attend any more of the sessions, even if they hold them." He was staring at the ash on the cigar now. "What was it at second?"

I frowned at him.

He said, "Why did they keep you on after this first kid was killed and the gag fell flat?"

"Oh," I said. "Well, they got serious by then; they thought maybe there really were aliens—"

"Crap," Tiny said deliberately.

I began to snap something back, but bit it off. "Yeah, I guess so," I said instead. "Anyway, they came to the same conclusion after the first day, so I'm clientless."

Tiny pointed the cigar at me. "Jeb, there's something screwy going on in the Scylla Club. There's a good reason for those killings, a damn good one."

Everybody wants to get in the act; everybody wants to be a detective and solve the big crime. "All right," I told him. "If you can figure it out, let the police know. It's driving them crazy. They can't figure out why any of the three should be killed. Nobody profits; there isn't any motive."

I finished that last over my shoulder as I wedged myself through the kids on my way out.

I walked down Green Avenue to Herkimer Boulevard, crossed to the other side and waited for the bus to City Center. I got out of the bus at West First and Herkimer and walked south to the Kroll Building. It didn't look any more attractive to me this morning than it ever did.

I went in and let a complaining Mike haul me up to the fifth floor. I unlocked the door to the office of *Lee and Knight, Private*

Investigations, tossed my hat to the dusty windowsill and sank into the swivel chair with a sigh.

After an interval, I fished the Kaywoodie out of the top drawer and loaded it. I waited until it was well lit and drawing nicely before I turned to the papers.

Tiny had been right. I'd got an awful razzing from the rags after the Holliday case, but nothing like this. They had to have somebody to hang it on, and I was it.

The phone rang and I picked it up and said, "Yeah? Jeb Knight speaking."

It was Marty Rhuling of the *Chronicle* and formerly of Army Intelligence and of the drinking team of Hermie Cain, Jeb Knight, and Marty Rhuling. He said, "Hey, Jeb, what's this about the police commission revoking your license?"

It took a moment for that to sink in. I said finally, "First I heard about it, Marty. Where'd you get it?"

"One of the boys on the police beat. Sure you can't tell me anything I could use, old comrade-in-arms?"

"No. No, I can't, Marty. My clients pulled me off the case yesterday, and like I said, I haven't heard anything about my license."

We insulted each other back and forth a while and he hung up.

I sat there staring at my further wall and at the license that proclaimed I was a private detective. That was what *it* said. I probably looked as though I was thinking, but I wasn't. My mind was as near to being a blank as a mind can get. Finally I got up from the swivel chair and reached for my hat.

I went down to the street and headed, on foot, north up West First to Lafayette, crossed the street and turned right to the Justice Building. I went in the front entrance this time, up the wide marble steps to the second floor and down the corridor to Davis's office.

Without knocking, I twisted the knob and stepped inside. Mike Quinn was sitting there, feet on the desk, a copy of *Amazing Stories* in his hand.

"Oh, *no,*" I protested. "You too?"

He looked up and grinned shamefacedly. "Hi, Buster." He indicated the magazine. "These stories ain't really so bad. I'm getting tired of westerns and sports."

"I'm surprised that with your sterling mentality you haven't tried the comic books," I told him. "Where's Davis?"

He ignored the crack. "He'll be back in a minute. Sit down, Buster. What goes?"

I took one of the battered straight chairs and sat down on it, reaching for my pipe.

"That's what I want to know," I told him.

Lieutenant Davis entered behind me. "Hello, Knight," he growled. There was an edge of truculence in his voice. He walked around behind his desk and took his chair.

I said, "One of the boys on the *Chronicle* says my license has been revoked." I loaded the pipe, then, remembering Davis's asthma, stuck it in my pocket. I had the feeling that I should be sore, but somehow I wasn't; somehow I didn't give a damn.

Davis said, "Look, Knight. You're probably all right as a guy. Some people figure that a private dick is a crook every time, kind of an occupational disease, like; but I never heard of your agency, back when Ken Lee was alive, or even since you took over, ever doing anything deliberately out of line. Your mistakes have probably all been honest ones."

"All right," I said, "I don't need the violins."

He leveled a pale thin finger at me. "Knight, you just aren't cut out for this game. I don't know how you ever got into it, but it's not for you. Take this Holliday deal, eh? A guy hires you to come to his house because he's afraid somebody'll take a crack at his wife's jewels. Why he doesn't call the police, I don't know. He calls you. The second night you're there, sure enough, a second story lad turns up. Everything gets exciting and what happens? The crook gets away with the jewels and you shoot your client in the leg."

I began to protest, but he cut me off.

"Yeah, I know," he went on. "You've got your side of the story and just why everything happened the way it did, but what I just said sums it up. Okay. Now then, you get into this deal with these science fiction nuts, and what happens? Two killings and an attempted killing go on right under your nose. You get under the feet of the men the department has working on the case, you even meddle around with bodies before the medical examiner sees them. All this time, you're taking money under false pretenses."

"Hey, wait a minute, here," I snapped, suddenly angry.

He shook his head emphatically. "Look, Knight. These two characters, Maddigan and Roget, hired you to check on the presence of aliens from space, eh? Nuts! You know they must have been all screwed up when they offered you that job. What sane man would hire a detective to go around tagging Martians?"

I growled, "Listen, I didn't want to take the damn job at first."

Mike Quinn grinned over at me. "They twist your arm, Buster?"

"Shut up, Mike." Davis shook his head negatively at me. "You even go to the point of using your personal friendship with a homicide detail man to stick your nose into affairs that have nothing to do with you."

I didn't like that. They'd evidently found that Hermie Cain had given me information. I wondered how much trouble he'd gotten into.

The lieutenant was shrugging. "At any rate, Knight, you're not cut out for this line of work. It isn't anything personal; like I said, you're probably a nice guy. *But you don't belong in the detective game.*" He was down-pitch in voice, very sincere. "The commission voted this morning to cancel your license; you'll probably be notified by mail today or tomorrow. There's some kind of deal under which you can request a hearing; frankly, I suggest you drop it."

I got to my feet. "All right, Davis," I said. "See you again sometime." I turned to go.

He said, "So long, Knight. Good luck, eh?"

Mike Quinn looked up at me embarrassedly, "Sorry, Buster," he said

"So long," I told him.

I felt like slamming it, but I closed the door quietly behind me and stood there in the corridor for a minute. Then I turned to the left and walked down to the office in which I'd seen Hermie Cain the day before.

He was there alone again, typing laboriously on an old Underwood. He looked up from it when I entered and grinned sourly at me; the grin went on and developed into the Cain yawn.

"Understand I got you into trouble, Herm," I began apologetically.

"Aw, it wasn't too bad," he said. "They raked me over the coals a little, that's all. Shucks, they can't do anything to me, Jeb; I gotta uncle on the commission."

I sat down on the edge of the desk, trying to think of something to say.

He yawned elaborately and resumed his careful pounding on the typewriter. "Heard you lost your license," he said. When I didn't answer, he added with studied off-handedness, "As a matter of fact, Jeb, it's probably just as well. You never did make much of a go at it."

"I'm getting tired of everybody telling me so," I said. "But probably you're right at that." I looked at the sheet he was typing. "Listen," I protested, "you don't have a ribbon in that typewriter."

"Haven't you ever seen anybody cut a mimeograph stencil before?" he asked, without taking his eyes from his work.

"Stencil?" I stared down at the sheet in his typewriter. "You mean to mimeograph you have to do one of those things for each page you want to run off?"

He yawned. "Sure, that's right."

Something was beginning to germinate. I said, "How many times can you use one of those stencil things?"

"Only once, what d'ya think? Once you cut a stencil, it's used."

"All right. Now, after you make this stencil and run off the copies you want, can you take the stencil out of the mimeograph machine and maybe use it again later on?"

"Sure, why not?" He yawned again and complained, "I gotta get more sleep nights."

"Listen, Herm, I'll see you later," I told him. "I just thought of something."

"Good enough, Jeb," he mumbled after me as I left the office. "See you later." He had bent back over his typewriter.

I hustled my way down the corridor to the steps and down them hurriedly and into the street. I hailed a cab, missed it, hailed another and got it. I snapped the driver the address of the Shulman home.

A little more than ten minutes later, the cab pulled up to 320 West Seventh and I got out and paid it off. The cab drove away and I stood there momentarily trying to figure out my approach. Finally I shrugged impatiently and started up the concrete walk. I'd just have to play it as it came.

I knocked on the side of the screen door and waited. It was all a carbon copy of my first visit. I could see her coming down the hallway from the kitchen toward me, her every appearance screaming *mother*. She was small, faded, gray; stamped with the perpetual tiredness of the proletarian housewife grown old in the perpetual search for security, in a world that has none to offer.

I said, "Good morning, Mrs. Shulman."

She squinted against the light of the sun and her tired eyes narrowed in an effort to place me.

I said, "I'm Jeb Knight, Mrs. Shulman. I was here the other day to ask you some questions about Harry."

She remembered. "Oh, yes. You were the one that wasn't really a policeman." She made no motion toward unlatching the screen.

I said nervously, "Listen, Mrs. Shulman. I wonder if I could speak to you again. Something new has developed, something that possibly, just possibly, might wind up all this."

She sighed. "The newspaper people and the officers have been here time and again, every day since—"

"Yes, of course," I hurried. "Actually, Mrs. Shulman, you don't have to talk to me if you don't wish. As they told you I'm not an officer. However, I do have something very important; something that might lead to Harry's murderer being apprehended."

She wiped her hands on her apron and blinked at me indecisively. It reminded me of her son.

I said, "Mrs. Shulman, do you realize the importance of the fact that all of Harry's most recent edition of his magazine were stolen?"

"I don't believe—"

"Mrs. Shulman," I pursued, "there was something in that issue that the murderer couldn't afford to have brought to light. He killed Harry, then destroyed all copies of his magazine, even one that I had in my desk."

She flicked the latch on the screen at last. "Come in, come in, Mr. Knight," she said. "I don't know what you want, but we can at least talk in comfort."

She led the way to the living room and settled herself in the uncomfortable-appearing easy chair and folded her hands in her lap. "Very well, very well, Mr. Knight. What did you want?" There was resignation in her voice.

I settled down on the couch, hat in hand, and tried to make my voice very sincere. "Mrs. Shulman, what did Harry do with his old stencils?"

"Stencils?"

"Those sheets he had to type up to make up his magazine."

"Oh, you mean for the mimeograph?"

"That's right. What did he do with them?" I was bending forward toward her in my excitement.

"Why, I don't know, Mr. Knight. I suppose that he threw them away."

I had a sinking feeling at that, but I said, "Listen, was there ever a time when Harry ran short of copies of his magazine and had to run off some more?"

She had to think about that for a minute. "Yes I believe there was. One time he had an article which stirred up quite a controversy. He had to go back and print another fifty copies."

My mouth was dry now. I said, "Mrs. Shulman, that means that he probably kept his stencils somewhere, filed them away."

She said, "Well, if he did, then they're in his files in the cellar. He never—"

"They're still there? His files are still in the cellar?"

"Why, yes. I've never touched a thing."

I came to my feet hurriedly. "Can't we go see?"

CHAPTER SEVENTEEN

THERE WERE TWENTY of them stashed away in a large brown Kraft envelope lettered "Stencils" with the current year on it. Those for the latest run-off of *Off-Trail Fantasy,* the September issue, were on the top, easily distinguishable.

My hand shook as I pulled them from the envelope. I turned and looked at Mrs. Shulman. "They're here," I told her in triumph. "We've got the material our murderer went to such pains to destroy."

She said nervously, "Perhaps I'd better call the police."

"Not yet," I told her. "Let me read it." I had to give her some excuse. "Possibly there'll be nothing of real interest to the police."

I looked around the cellar where Harry Shulman had made his "office," seeking a desk or table. It was fitted up almost exactly like Les Zimmer's with the exception that Zimmer had a complete printing outfit while Harry Shulman had been limited to a mimeograph machine.

She twisted her hands indecisively. "Well, if you think so." Then: "If you'd like we can go upstairs. The light would be better in the kitchen, I suppose."

The light was fine right here, but I followed her back up the cellar stairs and back to her large, spotlessly clean kitchen. In its center was a white, porcelain-topped table. I pulled up one of the red kitchen chairs and began scanning the stenciled page of contents. It wasn't too difficult to read the stencils—not as easy as a printed page, of course, but possible. It went:

Editorial
Fandom Can Be Fun, by Art Cole
This Month's Prozines, by Es Rapp
Wish I Had Written That, by A. E. Van Heinlein
Ultimate Destiny, by Harry Shulman
Insurgentism and the NFFF, by Vernon Briney
Book Nook, reviews, by Bob McCain

Mrs. Shulman was saying something about making coffee and I grunted a thanks, but my mind was on something else. I was trying to remember what Harry had told me about his magazine out there in the garden of Ross Maddigan's home. He'd wanted me to read something in particular. What was it?

I looked down at the table of contents again. Unless he had written some of the other pieces under a pen-name, there could be only two items of his: the editorial and the story, *Ultimate Destiny*. It seemed to me that the latter was the story he'd told me about. At any rate, it was as good a piece as any with which to start.

I turned the stencil pages to it and read:

~ ~ ~ ~ ~

ULTIMATE DESTINY

The second officer of the *Bright Star* looked at me quizzically. "Well," he said, "What do *you* think is the ultimate destiny of the human race?"

"Suicide," I told him.

He smiled, almost laughed. He was one of these big fellows, happy-go-lucky in appearance and more than ordinarily satisfied with the way of life. You don't see the type very often any more.

"How do you figure that?" he asked.

I said seriously, "One day soon, we will have realized all our ambitions and conquered our instincts. When those two points are reached, we'll see the futility of living; we'll end the farce, this ridiculous hoax."

"Go on," he said, but he was only half interested. His eye caught the two comets on his right sleeve, squinted critically; he lifted the arm to his mouth and breathed gently on the gold, then rubbed the sleeve on his left one.

"That's all," I said impatiently. "Man has been seeking what he misnames happiness ever since he has been man. His brain—obviously a result of a mutation nature should never have allowed—makes him the only animal capable of conceiving of such nonsense. The disillusionment will strike when he finally achieves his goal. He's nearing that point now."

The second officer still smiled. "Well, at least your ideas are unique."

That wasn't what I was trying to put over; I'm not interested in creating a new philosophy. "No, they aren't," I argued. "They're been stated a thousand times before. Take Omar, for instance; he saw the futility and committed suicide."

He rubbed his chin and looked as though he were trying to remember his schooling. "Omar Khayyam didn't commit suicide—did he?"

"Like *kert* he didn't; he committed suicide with a wine skin," I said emphatically. "The Rubaiyat was written after his pinnacle as a mathematician, astronomer and thinker. Remember where he says:

> *And much as Wine has play'd the Infidel,*
> *And robbed me of my Robe of Honor—Well,*
> *I Wonder often what the Vintners buy*
> *One half so precious as the stuff they sell.*

"Omar had already given up his so-called Robe of Honor when that was written," I finished.

The second officer considered that for a moment. "Maybe you're right about Omar Khayyam, but—well I wouldn't exactly consider it suicide." He looked very judicious.

"What would you call it, then?" I snapped. "What difference does it make if he slit his throat with a razor or if he spent the rest of his life sucking on bottles?"

"That's where your idea is wrong," he said. His eye had caught on the golden comets on his other sleeve and he went through the whole irritating process of polishing once again. "Even if mankind does become disillusioned, man won't commit mass suicide because he won't have the courage." He finished buffing his sleeve and smiled at me tolerantly, as though he'd just finished off my argument completely with that pearl of wisdom.

"You forget," I told him, "that I said he would also have to conquer his instincts." I was trying to hide my irritation. "Man is beginning to do that already. Every advance that science makes leads us further from our animal instincts. One day, perhaps, we'll even conquer the fear of death—*yes, one day we'll conquer the fear of death*—but *actually that isn't necessary.* Race suicide wouldn't have to entail shooting ourselves. We might take Omar's way out, or perhaps we would just stop having children. Notice that as a people grow more advanced, more sophisticated and educated, the birth rate falls off?"

He considered that a minute, taking a sip of his *woji* reflectively. "I don't think that man will ever run out of ambitions, to return to an earlier point you made," he said finally. "By the time one is conquered, another is created."

"You're wrong there," I told him decisively. "Our fundamental ambitions are simple ones and an increasingly large number are realizing them. We seek economic security, food, clothing and shelter, and the knowledge of freedom from want tomorrow. Then we seek a suitable mate, and, after that, or sometimes before, the applause of our fellows. Think it over, you'll find that's about all we seek."

"We seek the stars," he said dramatically. I shrugged in deprecation. "And have conquered them; and now what? That ambition of centuries is realized. After we first landed on Luna, the rest of it could be nothing but anticlimax. The thrill of touching a new planet, of reaching a new star system?" I shrugged again, contemptuously. "They're all monotonously alike, after all."

He went back again. "I don't see what's wrong about achieving these ambitions man has had."

"It isn't a matter of being wrong. It's just that when we've accomplished what we've always thought we needed to achieve happiness, the happiness isn't there— only disillusionment. Remember where Bobbie Burns says:

> *But pleasures are like poppies spread—*
> *You seize the flower, its bloom is shed;*
> *Or like the snowfall in the river,*
> *A moment white—then melts forever . . .*

The *Bright Star's* second officer grinned again. "I guess you think that Burns is another, like Omar Khayyam, who found that when you achieve what you want you might as well bump yourself off."

"That's right," I answered him, ignoring his sarcasm. "It's the *pursuit* of happiness that counts; not the alleged happiness itself. The goal, actually, is never reached; there is no such thing as happiness. Man comes nearest to it only when he seeks the hardest and *seems* on the verge of attainment. When we finally find out, as a race, that happiness is nonexistent, that's when the blow-off will come.

"You'll notice, by the way," I added, "that in the Declaration of Independence, Jefferson says, 'Life, Liberty, and the Pursuit of Happiness.' He doesn't say *happiness,* but the *pursuit of happiness.* He was well aware of the fact that it was a goal impossible to attain."

He finished his drink. "Well, I don't believe we'll have to worry about it for a time; suicide, I mean. By the way things look, it'll be a long stretch before the human race realizes its ambitions."

I said, "Not so long as you might think. Already we've reached the point where we've achieved security. We've built a productive industrial machine which will do all the work necessary to create luxury for all. We've ended war, finally. Yes, we have the peace and security man has sought for so long. It won't be long now before man finds he's through."

He stirred restlessly. "Well, so far only Omar and Burns and Jefferson have felt the way you do. I'm glad the theory isn't more widespread." He stood up.

"I didn't say they were the only ones," I denied. "It's just that they've been articulate. I wonder sometimes about their desire to write about it after they saw the futility. Most just find out that nothing, after all, makes any difference, and stop doing anything."

I had talked too long. I could see he was getting tired of the conversation. "Listen," I said, trying to keep the urgency from my voice, "how about another *woji?* All this talking has made me a little dry."

"Sure," he said and slid a two-minute credit out to Beri. Then he walked over to the Vio-Box and looked over its selection. I could see he was tired of listening to me; he wouldn't be back. I drank the *woji* as slowly as I could, trying to stretch it out.

Beri leaned over the bar directly across from me. "I don't know why in *kert* I let a makron like you hang out in here," he shrilled. "You'd talk the ear off a brass Mercurian *Bouncer.* You got the wrong tactics for a moocher, that's all. Why in *kert* don't you let the other guy do the talking? You'd get a lot more drinks that way."

"Beri," I told him, "you're a peasant, a Venusian peasant. Look, how about letting me have another *woji* until tomorrow? I've got a little job coming up that will net me at least a few hour credits."

Beri laughed.

~ ~ ~ ~ ~

When I'd finished it, I skimmed through again, just in case. The story was all right, not professional, really, but passable; in fact, better than you'd have thought an amateur would be turning out. This couldn't be it; there was nothing here that would push a man to murder.

Mrs. Shulman had finished preparing the coffee, and set a cup next to me and a plate of cookies in the table's center.

She said hesitantly, "Did you find what you were looking for?"

I shook my head. "Not yet, but it must be in here."

I started at the beginning and read the editorial. It was principally a complaint about people who joined fan clubs for reasons other than an actual understanding and love of science fiction. It pointed out cases of girls who had joined for the social life, of professionals who joined for business purposes, and so forth. Harry—assuming that it was Harry who had written it—wound up with a stirring call for the elimination of all fans who didn't love fandom for fandom's sake.

It couldn't be that. It came to me suddenly that the item to which the killer objected didn't necessarily have to be from Harry's pen. Possibly it was included in the piece of some other amateur author. I read every word the issue contained, fiction, articles, book reviews, magazine reviews; I even studied the two cartoons.

I didn't get anything out of any of them.

Something was wrong here. I sat back in my chair and stared down at the stencils. There wasn't anything in this magazine that would point the finger of suspicion at Harry Shulman's killer. I tugged at an ear in exasperation. There was something definitely wrong, and I couldn't quite get it.

Mrs. Shulman said wearily, "You didn't find it, did you?"

I shook my head at her.

She had been sitting across from me, quietly watching as I went through the stencils. Now she sighed and came to her feet. "I suppose I should get about my work."

"Listen, Mrs. Shulman," I told her, "you should get in touch with the police about this. They might find something I've missed." I paused, then, slowly, "I'm not really a very good detective, myself."

"Very well," she said emotionlessly. "I'll phone them. Should I say that you discovered the stencils?"

I lifted my right shoulder in a disheartened shrug. "It doesn't make much difference."

I took up my hat from where I'd tossed it on an empty chair and banged it against my leg once or twice. "Thanks for the coffee—and the cooperation, Mrs. Shulman. I thought I had something, evidently I didn't."

She followed me to the door and told me goodbye. I walked down the concrete sidewalk to the street and looked back. I could see her small figure behind the screen, watching after me. The newspapers had said she had no relatives, now that Harry was dead. I wondered how she made her living. It hadn't been any too ample a one even before, while her son was alive and working, from the appearance of the home.

I walked down West Seventh to Montgomery, passing within a couple of hundred feet of the Zimmer home. There was a police car parked in front of it, complete with two uniformed cops. They looked me over carefully as I walked by. Evidently Zimmer was in more of a dither than ever.

At the boulevard, I took a bus downtown, my mind still a vacuum. Somewhere in here there had to be some sense. There had to be.

I went down Montgomery to East First and transferred there to the Brentwood bus and rode it south to Burr Avenue. Sam's Bar was just two buildings down.

CHAPTER EIGHTEEN

I HAD A NUMBER of beers at Sam's and walked on up to my office. The prehistoric elevator took me to the fifth floor and I walked down the hallway to the dingy door that says, *Lee and Knight, Private Investigations.* I unlocked the door and went in.

Without taking off my hat, I sat down at the desk and reached for the phone. I remembered the number from the last time. I dialed and had Mrs. Shulman on the wire in less than a half-minute.

I said, "Mrs. Shulman, this is Jeb Knight again. I think I've found the answer to the question that wasn't in Harry's magazine."

She said something I didn't quite get.

I said, "Mrs. Shulman, you mentioned that Harry was treasurer of the Scylla Club. Could you tell me if he kept the club's books there at the house?"

"Why, I believe so."

"I wonder if you could look them up and find out just how much money the club has in the treasury?"

She hesitated for a long moment. I was having to sell her all over again every time we came in contact.

"This is very important, Mrs. Shulman," I pressed.

"Well, it might take a little while, Mr. Knight. Should I phone you back?"

I gave her my number and gently replaced the receiver in its cradle. I took my pipe from my pocket and stared at it, not able to decide whether or not I wanted to smoke.

I had a small tin of aromatic tobacco in one of the desk drawers. I searched it out and filled up with it. Usually I don't smoke aromatic blends; they pall on me too fast. One pipe load goes well enough, but I can seldom get through a whole tin. I struck a match, lit the pipe carefully, puffed two or three times, then blew out the match and tossed it to the ash tray.

The pipe was nearly finished by the time the phone rang again. It was Mrs. Shulman.

She said, "Mr. Knight, I found the book in which Harry kept his reports. The treasury was three dollars and fifteen cents."

I asked her one other question, thanked her and then hung up.

I stared at the phone for another ten minutes, then dug a phone book from a drawer and flopped it down on my blotter. I looked up the number I wanted and then dialed again. I didn't place the voice that answered, so I said. "Is Les Zimmer there?"

"Did you want Lester Zimmer Senior, or Lester Zimmer Junior?"

I wanted Lester Zimmer Junior and waited while he was called. Evidently Ma and Pa Zimmer had returned from their vacation. I wondered what the old man, who was such a nut about fireproofing, thought of the burn on the wall.

Zimmer's thin voice said hello.

I said, "Zimmer, this is Jeb Knight. I wanted to ask you something."

He began, "Mr. Knight, I read in the paper that—"

"Listen," I interrupted, "all I want to know is what Art Roget does for a living."

He stuttered something, finally clearing it up until I could understand, "I—well—I think Art works in an electrical supply house. He's a clerk or something."

"You wouldn't know how much he makes?"

"No, Mr. Knight, I—"

"I'll get in touch with you later." I thought a minute, then added. "Listen, Zimmer, you can stop worrying about being killed. You'll be all right."

He wanted to shrill some more questions at me, but I cut him short, put my finger on the cut-off bar and left it there while I thought up the next move. I let it up and dialed again.

She wasn't at her apartment hotel; I should have known she wouldn't be. I looked up Brandenburg and Sons in the book and dialed again.

The PBX operator told me hello and I asked for Julie Sharp.

Julie said, "Yes?"

"This is Jeb Knight, Miss Sharp."

"Hello, Jeb." There was a soft warmth in her voice that I liked. "The name is Julie."

"Julie," I said, "I think maybe things are making sense at last. You told me something the other day that didn't sink in at the time. I wanted to check back with you. All right?"

There was an infinitesimal disappointment in her voice. "What was it about, Jeb?"

I told her and got her to repeat, as nearly as she could, what she'd said. Then I asked, "Another thing, I'd forgotten but now I recall that I told you about Harry Shulman giving me a copy of his fanzine. Did you repeat that fact to anyone; did you tell anyone I had a copy of it in my desk?"

She gave me the answer I'd expected.

Ross Maddigan was next. I had to try three different calls before locating him. When I did, my questions irritated him, which wasn't surprising, and he finally hung up on me. But once again, the answers I did get were the ones I'd figured upon.

I couldn't locate Art Roget, and I couldn't get Sandra Maddigan, but I had a sneaking suspicion that wherever she was Rog Craig wasn't far off.

I spent another hour staring at the walls. For once, I was thinking. I put my feet up on the desk blotter and smoked until smoking no longer meant anything. Then I took my feet down, adjusted my hat and headed for the door.

The elevator took me to the street and I walked up to the cab stand on Marion and West Second and got a checker. I gave the driver the address of Maddigan and Maddigan and relaxed, my mind blank once again, while the cab took me there.

The offices of Maddigan and Maddigan were on the third floor. I took the elevator up, asked the boy what direction the concern was, in the labyrinth of halls, and had it pointed out to me.

The office suite wasn't particularly large, but it was well done. In the outer office were four girls, one of them operating a PBX. There were three inner offices opening off the large one. I could see the name, *James L. Maddigan,* and *President, Private* on one of them.

I said to the girl at the PBX, "I'm Jeb Knight. I'd like to talk to Mr. Maddigan."

"Do you have an appointment?" I recognized the voice from the times I'd talked to her on the phone. Her business suit was severely cut, she was small, washed out, and she'd spent too many years at a job that at best was monotonous; she looked as though she'd given up the dream of a home and family.

I shook my head. "But he'll see me."

She placed plugs and switched switches and said something to which I didn't bother to listen. She looked back up at me, frowning apologetically. "I'm sorry, Mr. Maddigan says that he's too busy right now, Mr. Knight. He wanted me to tell you that you should bill him for the remainder of your fee."

garden. He was taken—probably without argument on his part—to a tall building, perhaps five minutes' fast drive from Ross's home, and pushed from it to fall to his death. The murderer then went down, wrapped the body in a tarpaulin or something, and took it back to the party, back through the hedge to the dark spot where we found it. I doubt that they were gone more than twenty minutes—not long enough for anyone to notice their absence. The killer probably had the cold-blooded gall to leave the tarpaulin in his car; taking the chance that it wouldn't be searched. It wasn't."

Maddigan said, "It makes sense thus far. It sounds like a logical explanation; in fact, I understand that the police have already considered the theory. But what did you say was the motive?"

I shook my head. "Not yet; I'll get to that. Two days later Les Zimmer was doped. He slept extremely soundly under the influence of the narcotic. While he slept, the murderer entered the Zimmer house, using a key he had secured previously with this plan in mind, and came up to Zimmer's room. The murderer had an ordinary blowtorch. He went to work on the wall, creating, as best he could, the effect that would result from one of the futuristic 'heat rays,' as Les called it. If he had wanted to kill Zimmer, he could have. He didn't."

Maddigan was scowling at me again. "That sounds possible, Knight, but highly improbable. Once again, *why?*" He leaned forward, took hold of his knee caps and squeezed.

"In a moment. That's the important point; and we'll get to it. Next on the list was Bob Carr. It didn't have to be him; it could have been almost any other fan at the convention who was unknown to the murderer. But Carr was particularly good because of his knowledge of extra-terrestrial gobbledygook; that helped the misdirection."

"Unknown to him? Are you jesting, Knight? Are you implying that—"

"Let me tell it my way, Mr. Maddigan. As I said, this is in the way of a final report. I think it's accurate. What you do afterwards, how you act on it, is your business, but you've paid for this and I'll give it to you."

Maddigan shifted in his chair and went back to his cigar, but his facial expression told me he wasn't taking it all.

"All right," I continued. "The murderer dressed himself in a costume which completely disguised him, got the key to Ross's room from the clerk, approached Bob Carr and, using some excuse, got him to go to Ross's room. Our murderer was carrying a suitcase. In it was various equipment he needed. I'm not sure just what he did use; for one thing he probably had some type of elctrical transformer to step up the hotel's current so that he could get a sufficient shock to kill Carr.

"That isn't important for this report; undoubtedly the police will work it out later. Our murderer had another piece of equipment in his suitcase, too, but we'll get to that. Sufficient now to say that he killed Carr and dragged him into the corridor and left him there."

Maddigan rubbed a hand up and down his right thigh impatiently. "You still haven't arrived at the motivation, Knight. How did this mysterious person of yours profit by his homicides and by this fantastic scene at the home of Les Zimmer?"

I said softly, "He didn't, Mr. Maddigan. Thus far, the murderer hasn't profited at all by the killings that have taken place. His plan was to profit by the *next* killing. As I said earlier, all this has been misdirection."

He sat quietly, his eyes on my face but seemingly going beyond it and into infinity.

I went on wearily, "The oldest of police theorems, Mr. Maddigan, is *find the motive.* Given the motive for a crime, you can usually find your criminal. For instance, if a man carrying heavy life insurance in his wife's name dies of poisoning, the obvious first suspect is his wife. So obvious that even though she may have built up a seemingly foolproof alibi, the police are usually able to break it down. They have the motive—they can find the criminal.

"That was what our killer had to avoid. He badly wanted to kill a certain person, but he knew that if he did, the finger of suspicion would point immediately to him. He alone had motive.

"So he started his chain of misdirection. He killed two persons wantonly, without reason, deliberately choosing two whose deaths would profit no one. He took steps to see the case would be publicized and that the fact that they were motiveless and fantastic would be stressed. He was building up a situation, so that when the third killing took place, it too would be thought of as motiveless. Whether or not it would have worked, I don't know. Perhaps. Whether or not a touch of insanity was necessary in order to be capable of such wanton killing, I don't know either."

"Ridiculous," Maddigan blurted, getting chilly about the eyes.

I lifted my right shoulder, let it drop. "I don't think so. It's the only answer to the whole thing."

"Well, who is this third victim? Who is it that is next on the list?"

"Your nephew, Ross."

CHAPTER NINETEEN

WE SAT THERE in a silence you could emotionally feel, for long moments. James Maddigan extinguished his cigar carefully, leaned back in his chair and crossed his hands over his stomach. He worked his plump lips in and out, as though undecided what to say.

Finally, "Evidently, you have a good deal more. You might as well proceed."

"All right. Let's go back to the beginning again. You must have decided a long time ago to kill Ross. The reason?" I shrugged. "I'm not sure. Either you were misappropriating his funds and were afraid he would discover the fact, or possibly you were jealous of your wife's attentions to him; maybe both."

Maddigan's eyes flared suddenly. "Leave my wife out of this discussion, Knight! Continue with your silly jabber, if you must, but leave Sandra out of it! Do you understand?"

"All right. I won't mention your wife again. To go on: You initiated the idea of hiring me to investigate the possibility of the presence of alien life forms. That was the beginning of the misdirection. You brought Art Roget and Harry Shulman along with you so that it would look as though it were a three man idea. It wasn't. Neither Roget nor Shulman nor the treasury of the Scylla Club had sufficient funds to hire me. It was your scheme from the beginning.

"At the Scylla Club party, you talked Shulman into accompanying you and drove him to your own home, only a few minutes away by car. I'm not sure of this, but it seems likely."

He sat there staring at me, wordless.

"You pushed him from the terrace of your apartment into the shaded and dark courtyard below. It wasn't too difficult to do. Then you retrieved his body and returned with it to the party.

"You had undoubtedly been preparing for this for some time. Somewhere along the line in your activities in the Scylla Club, you were able to acquire a key to Zimmer's house. I don't know how—I don't care. You got it, knowing how you were going to use it. I admit, I might be wrong here; you might be an accomplished amateur locksmith, which would also explain how you entered my office to secure the fanzine from my desk.

"The day following Shulman's death Zimmer came to your home to protest your hiring me. You took advantage of the opportunity and slipped him a mickey. When he got home that night, unknowingly drugged, you knew he'd sleep through your entering his house and applying your blowtorch to his wall."

Maddigan yawned deliberately. "You know, Knight, you've constructed quite a story, but you miss one point. Don't you realize that *you* are my best alibi? Don't you recall that only a few minutes before your discovery of the body of Bob Carr you'd been talking to me over the phone? I called you from here, my office, a full half-hour away from the Bigelow Hotel."

I grinned sourly at him. "I'll admit that had me stumped. But I finally figured it out. That phone call wasn't made from your office; it was made from Ross's room where you had just finished off the Carr boy. I know it *sounded* as though you were in your office. I could even hear the typewriters in the background, and, of course, your office girl's voice. But remember, I told you that our murderer had two machines in his suitcase? One was a recorder, probably a wire recorder. On the wire you had your office girl's voice and the typewriters' clicking. You must have made the recording one day through your own phone. At any rate, at the time of Carr's death you simply called me from Ross's room, let me listen momentarily to your recording, then cut in direct and carried on with the conversation."

I pointed to a door that opened upon the corridor. "You'd probably left your office by that rear door there, telling your girls not to bother you. You went down to the convention—somewhere along the line getting into that Martian costume—committed your murder, then returned to the office. Later, you went out by the front entrance, letting the employees see you go and giving them the impression that you'd been in the whole period."

Maddigan was still trying to bluff it through. He said, "If all this were true, Knight, why in the world would I hire you? Would I be so stupid as to—"

"You had two reasons," I said bitterly, "neither of them flattering to me. For one thing, you wanted to get started with this aliens from space stuff, one of the principal ingredients of your campaign of misdirection, and you assumed that no other agency would take the job. For another, you wanted a line on the police. One of the things you asked me first was whether or not I had connections on the police force. You wanted daily reports. Sure you did; you wanted to know how the cops were coming along, and you figured I'd be able to help you there. I was. I got dope from Hermie Cain, a wartime buddy, and passed it on to you.

"You weren't afraid of me. You knew I was the most incompetent detective in the city; that's another reason I was hired rather than someone else. I should have been suspicious of that from the beginning."

He eyed me coldly now. "What in the world started you on this trend of thought, Knight?"

It was about over. I said wearily, "I got an idea from Harry Shulman's magazine. Stealing them—you must have picked up a key from Harry sometime or other, too—was another piece of misdirection, because, actually, there was nothing in that issue of which you were afraid. Nevertheless, his editorial gave me a hint. You were in the Scylla Club for another reason than science fiction. You've shown a dozen times that you have no real interest in science fiction; not even the books in your home are science fantasy.

"Your real reason for joining the Scylla Club was to be near Ross. Julie Sharp told me that you and he didn't particularly get along, but you needed a way of getting close to him so you could find a favorable opportunity for murder."

James L. Maddigan came to his feet and stared down at me. "You realize that you can't prove any of this."

I stood up too. "I admit that, Mr. Maddigan. I can't prove it at all; but, for that matter, I don't have to. I told you at the beginning that the police could ferret out murderers better than can a private detective. They can and will; it isn't my problem. All they need is the hint I stumbled upon. When they start checking back they'll be able to find the necessary evidence."

"What, for instance?" he sneered.

I was tired of talk now, and winding up. "Possibly the day you went to the Bigelow Hotel and killed Carr, someone spotted you along the way. Possibly your office girl, outside, will remember that you made no phone call from the office at the time you were supposedly talking to me from here. Possibly—possibly a lot of things. As I said, the police will be better at this than I could hope to be."

I finished wearily, "I guess that's all, Mr. Maddigan. That's all of my report." I turned my back to him and started for the door.

He snarled, "Wait! Wait a minute! Let me think."

I looked back and shook my head negatively. "It's no good, Mr. Maddigan; you've got no out. You can't even kill me here, because your office girl saw me enter. Besides that, I phoned the police; they'll be on their way over now."

All the fight was out of him suddenly. His heavy shoulders sagged. He began desperately, "Perhaps we could—"

I shook my head again. "It's no go. Even if I was a potential blackmailer, I'd be afraid. You're too clever, Maddigan, to allow a blackmailer to have something on you. And too utterly ruthless. Oh, I don't really believe you're insane, not in the ordinary sense of the word. You don't have to be insane to be a killer of persons who have harmed you not at all. You just have to be ruthless, completely so.

"No, I won't blackmail you, Maddigan. The minute we'd made a deal you'd start figuring a way of eliminating me. Besides that, the racket doesn't appeal to me. I'll admit that you've managed to finish off my last chances of making a success of my detective business; there might be an ironic twist in your setting me up as a blackmailer. But, somehow or other, I'm going to appreciate seeing you pay for Harry Shulman's death."

I left then, closing the door softly behind me.

The office girl smiled brightly and said, "Good afternoon, Mr. Knight."

"Good afternoon," I told her.

I met Lietuenant Davis at the elevators. He came charging out, his face pale with rage, and nearly bumped into me.

He saw who it was, did a double take that would have done credit to a Walt Disney cartoon, and checked his rush. Mike Quinn, more easily, came ambling out of the elevator after him.

Davis snapped, "Okay, wise guy; you can't stay out of it, can you? You can't keep your nose where it belongs, eh? I'm placing you under arrest for—"

I shook my head at him. "Shut up, Davis," I said. "In the first place, as I told Quinn, I haven't been officially notified as yet that my license has been revoked—"

His mouth dropped open at the snarl in my voice, but he snapped it shut preparatory to starting roaring again.

"Besides," I went on, before he caught his breath, "I've just located your killer for you."

Mike Quinn laughed. "Oh, brother! Listen to Buster."

Davis spun on him. "Shut up, Mike; I'll handle this." Then back to me. "What're you talking about, eh?" He had sneering disbelief in his voice, but there was also desperate hope in his eyes. It suddenly came to me that I probably wasn't the only one taking an awful panning as a result of this case.

I motioned with my thumb toward Maddigan's door. "There he is, James L. Maddigan; he's your boy."

He snapped, "What evidence do you have for that crazy charge?"

"That's your business, Davis; I'm just giving you a tip. You can work it out, and you can get the credit. But I can suggest two things to check for a beginning. First, the books of Maddigan and Maddigan. He's probably been stealing Ross Maddigan blind. The second thing to check is his relation with his wife. He's crazy jealous of her and she's been playing up to his nephew—among others."

"But why the devil would he—"

"Listen, Davis," I said wearily. "I've just been through all this; I'm not going to do it again. He was dragging a whole fishing boat of red herring all over the place, preparatory to killing Ross. Check the back of his car for bloodstains he might have got carrying Shulman around the night of the first death. Another thing: he claims he phoned me from his office; I think he did it from Ross's room at the Bigelow. But this is your job, as you've told me a hundred times. Why should I work it out for you?"

He was staring at me, silently now. Then he said slowly, "I think you're nuts, but we'll follow it up— we're following everything up in this case, just on the off chance that we'll find the faintest lead." His voice went a degree softer. "You've taken a working over on this, Knight, but if it works out—" He rubbed the back of his neck with slow care.

"I know; you'll see I get my license back," I sneered. "And what good would it do me? My reputation wasn't bad enough before, I have to wind up with my latest client being the killer in the most sensational murder case this town's seen in years. Some chance, after that, I'd have of getting clients."

I turned from them and entered the elevator cage. The operator had been standing there, watching us, wide-eyed.

Mike Quinn opened his mouth to say something.

I snarled, "And if you call me Buster just once more I'll bust you in the trap!"

He blinked his eyes and his mouth snapped shut.

"Lobby," I growled to the operator.

I walked out to the street and located a cab to take me back to the office. I felt washed out.

There was a solitary letter under the door of the offices of *Lee and Knight, Private Investigations.* The envelope was an official one, from the commissioner of police. I didn't bother to open it.

I looked up at the calendar. It told me I had two more days' rent paid. This whole thing hadn't *really* made any difference, anyway. I'd been figuring on giving it all up that day when the three of them had first entered.

I got an empty cardboard carton out of the closet and placed it on top of the desk. I opened the top drawer and began pulling out papers, old letters, office supplies and the odds and ends that had accumulated in the past months. From the top of the desk I took my ashtray, emptied it into the wastebasket, then tossed it after the rest into the carton. Two pencils and the small green desk blotter followed. I didn't know what in Mars I wanted *that* for, but in it went.

I opened the second drawer and began cleaning it out. I found the pocket knife I'd lost two weeks ago.

The phone rang stridently.

I looked at it for a minute, then picked it up. "Jeb Knight," I grunted.

"Jeb? This is Julie." There was excitement in her voice.

"Hello, Julie," I said emotionlessly.

"Have you heard the news?"

"Maybe. I don't know. What news?"

"James Maddigan has committed suicide. He left a note—"

"Yeah," I muttered, "so he found his *Ultimate Destiny,* uh?"

"I beg your pardon?"

"Nothing;" I told her. "The name of a story Harry Shulman wrote. Did Maddigan confess to the two killings?"

There was surprise now. "That's right. How did you know?"

I said softly, "I talked him into it. They wouldn't have been able to hang it on him; not in a hundred years."

She was saying something else that I didn't get. I was thinking of Harry Shulman's mother, standing there at the screen door watching after me as I left.

Then I caught her words again. There was warmth in her voice and she was saying, "What about that date you were talking about, Jeb? A girl can't just sit by her telephone night after night waiting for you to call, you know." There was laughter in her voice, but something else, too.

I said flatly, "Maybe some other time, Julie. Maybe I'll give you a ring."

She didn't say anything. I put the receiver back on the crossbar of the telephone cradle.

I said out loud, "What darn good would a guy like me be for Julie? No job, no money, no future—no ambition. She's a damn sight better off with Ross Maddigan."

I looked down at my packing and growled, "I can do this tomorrow."

I put my hat on the back of my head, stuck my hands in my pockets and started off for Sam's, not bothering to close the door behind me.

THE END

AFTERWORD

CITIZEN OF THE WORLD

Dallas McCord "Mack" Reynolds was a very special person, or perhaps I should say half a person. Solidly integrated with his wife of many years, Jeanette, the two of them became fabulously interconnected as one inseparable entity . . . an iconic citizen of the world.

Mack had nothing even vaguely related to a "normal" upbringing. From his infancy he was thoroughly programmed to be a worker for the Socialist Labor Party. Mack's father, Verne Reynolds, was a high-placed member of that organization and, seemingly, a perennial candidate for President of the USA. From the age of seven, Mack traveled with his father and made encouraging speeches, urging audiences to "Vote for my daddy" at every stop.

He was destined to be "different" and to spend most of his time traveling, desperately seeking a place he could feel at home . . . a composure he could never feel within the USA.

In 1950, Jeanette, calling on her Amerind background, suggested that they try living in Taos, New Mexico, where they found a small farm adjacent to the Taos Indian Reservation and settled in for a while with other writers and artists struggling to make their own futures secure. Among them were Walt Sheldon and Fredric Brown, who became fast friends and encouragers. Especially Fredric Brown, who spent much time with Dallas, drinking and talking shop, encouraging Dallas to work at fiction writing in a professional manner.

It was then that Mack began writing seriously, forcing himself to write at least six pages of manuscript every day. Ten pages would have placed him among current professional writers, but Mack wanted to be slow and sure, so he took his time with his own prose. There was no upper limit on the amount of pages he could turn out, but he forced himself to produce those six manuscript pages each day, writing in the early mornings. Writing what he thought he should be writing, mystery fiction.

When Fredric Brown pointed out to him that it was obvious Dallas was a reader of science fiction, therefore he should be writing science fiction, and not detective fiction. . . the ghost of Jules

Verne, Mack's father's namesake, finally claimed his projected victim.

In 1949 Mack Reynolds wrote "Last Warning," his first science fiction story and, much to his surprise, sold it right away to *Planet Stories*. And then something unknown happened and the story wasn't published in *Planet Stories,* one of those odd situations where an editor accepts a submission, the author is paid, but the story somehow falls between the cracks and never makes it into the magazine. "Last Warning" remained unpublished for many years, finally appearing in the NESFA collection *Compounded Interest* in 1983.

Also in 1949 Fredric Brown's *What Mad Universe* was published. It was an instant classic of science-fiction-fan-related fiction, and one that inspired Mack Reynolds, because of his close friendship with fellow Taosian Brown, to emulate his work. It took him two years to write his counter to Brown's novel, and Mack's *The Case of the Little Green Men* was published in 1951, also becoming an instant classic of science-fiction-fan-related fiction.

In 1950, before Mack's *The Case of the Little Green Men* was published, he finally sold his first published science fiction short story, "Isolationist." It appeared in *Fantastic Adventures* for June. After his disappointment with "Last Warning," Mack finally felt as if he was about to hit is stride in the field of science fiction.

~ ~ ~ ~ ~

In *The Expatriates* (Regency Books, 1963), Mack Reynolds wrote:

> "It was in Paris that Garry Davis originally hit his stride, proclaiming himself to be the first 'Citizen of the World.' He renounced his American citizenship and called for those of good will to do likewise. Art Buchwald, in one of his amusing *New York Herald-Tribune* columns, recounts the early days of the Gary Davis 'movement' when Buchwald, among other veterans of the war living on a G.I. student income, set to work to turn out circulars on a mimeograph machine and to help distribute them, mail them and answer letters of inquiry. By Buchwald's account, it must have been fun at the time. . . .
>
> "When we met Garry Davis, it was at a science fiction convention in Chicago in 1952. An actor by profession, he put on a skit involving an absent-minded professor splitting an atom, and was quite the success of the evening."

And I was there as well, hiding in the crowds watching Garry Davis perform on stage. It was my first science fiction WorldCon, but not my last. I had already met numbers of the professionals and fans before that convention, but it was there at ChiCon II that Mack Reynolds and I first met. It was altogether an insignificant happening and one that would have been easily forgotten by both of us had it not, fortunately, signaled the beginning of a true friendship that would, in time, span decades.

~ ~ ~ ~ ~ ~

In 1963 I had been working as an editor for William Hamling's Blake Pharmaceuticals front for his pornography novels for two years. During that time, Mack was writing a series of travel articles for Hamling's men's magazine, *Rogue*, and I read every one of those columns with growing envy, as well as Mack's private correspondence with the Greenleaf gang. And, by attrition, I was about to become editor in chief of those sleazebooks.

As part of the publishing front, under the name of Regency Books, we occasionally published "clean" books and it was my pleasure and delight to edit Mack Reynolds's *The Expatriates*. I wrote about this extensively and told how very much Mack Reynolds and his wanderlust had influenced my life and how Mack, personally and directly, had added to my own desires to travel and experience things beyond my imagination.

The Expatriates was partly a collection of Mack's memories of traveling all around the world looking for the perfect place for him and Jeanette to live. It was also a list of the negatives associated with living in the USA that Mack found impossible to tolerate, as did many of the countless thousands of US expatriates living in far-flung countries everywhere.

In this book Mack poured out his heart, hammering away at the things that most disturbed him about living in the USA. . . the brainwashing and double-think constantly force-fed to the citizens, turning them into docile, compliant workers for the industries that owned the professional politicians who were allegedly supposed to be looking out for and protecting those compliant workers.

Chief among Mack's personal hatreds were the omnipresent racial standards forcing many groups to live far below the commonplace standards and to be constantly put down for their race or their color. Mack even felt that he and Jeanette were discriminated against in some US states where it was forbidden for mixed races to become married. . . this because of Jeanette's Amerind (native American Indian) background.

The next worst hate was the way people in the USA who did not conform to religious imposed heterosexuality were treated, even beaten and left on the streets to die. There were no provisions for homosexuality at all, gay or Lesbian, and neither would be tolerated even though both were commonplace throughout the nation.

Another of Mack Reynolds' crusades was to try to bring the US into conformity with other nations as far as personal use of recreational drugs was concerned. His comments in *The Expatriates* were:

"Throughout the world, among civilized peoples, the narcotics addict is recognized as a sick man. In the United States, addicts are criminals to be imprisoned.

"The line drawn between what a narcotic is and what it isn't seems an arbitrary one. In the United States, caffeine in coffee, tea, Coca-Cola, and Pepsi-Cola is perfectly legal. For that matter, it can be purchased in 'No-Doz' tablets in drug stores and even truck-stop restaurants along the highways without prescription. Tobacco is also openly available, in spite of recent claims of smoking being conducive to lung cancer. According to Norman *The Naked and the Dead* Mailer, who has self-admittedly done considerable research in the field, the cigarette habit is harder to shake than is heroin. We wouldn't know.

"Marijuana, on the other hand, is illegal.

"Back in the thirties a scandal arose about American soldiers stationed in the Panama Canal Zone smoking marijuana. After numerous letters of indignation to newspapers and magazine articles viewing with alarm, the Surgeon General of the U.S. Army did an editorial on the subject for the Army medical journal. In it, rather testily, he declared that marijuana wasn't any more dangerous than cigarettes and, in fact, wasn't habit-forming. A few years later, a similar cry went up in New York, and Mayor LaGuardia named a commission to investigate the use of the weed. To everyone's surprise, including LaGuardia's and the commissioners, they found that marijuana is not habit-forming, is not a sexual stimulant, and is not conducive to crime. They could have saved themselves a considerable amount of time had they read the definitive work on the subject, a several-volume report of a British commission in India, brought out during the nineteenth century. The whiskey people in Scotland had complained about the wide use of 'bhang' or Indian hemp. Investigation brought out the above information. Not habit-forming, not a sexual stimulant, not conducive to crime.

"The question becomes, then, why is marijuana listed as a narcotic and its use or possession a prison offense? Sponsors of the weed claim that the reason is because the stuff cannot be taxed efficiently, were it legal. It is unbelievably easy to raise, will grow in just about any climate, and anyone can cure his own. Its effect is similar to that of alcohol, except there is little, if any, hangover. In short, there is no profit in it for the equivalent of tobacco firms and distillers, and the government's liquor taxes would plummet if it became widely used.

"Be that as it may, there is no doubt that American narcotics laws tend to drive our addicts abroad, both for a source of supply and to avoid prison, rather than to cure them."

~ ~ ~ ~ ~

In 1966, thanks mostly to Donald Gilmore and the incredible pornography empire he was building for himself in Guadalajara, I began to feel the need to expand into Mexico myself. With Don's help I found the perfect house in Ajijic, Jalisco, and by early 1967 it had been reconstructed to my design, including the addition of a guest room on the upper deck. All the renovations had been completed, the interior redecorated and furnished, the yard landscaped, and the house staffed. And, in order to be closer to the core of porno writers turning out many manuscripts every month for Greenleaf Classics (we were publishing *fifty* titles a month at the time), I became an expatriate myself and moved into the middle of that porno factory.

That house, at *Constitution 14,* became in short order *la casa de me corizon. . .* the place where my heart lived. And where I lived for five and a half years. . . the very best five and a half years of my entire life. The first time, ever, that I felt really free and unrestricted by the continuous brainwashing by USA feds and their multinational owners. Mack Reynolds was right all along, and he gave me the right to feel as free as he and Jeanette did.

While I lived there in Ajijic, only a few hours away from the Reynolds in San Miguel de Allende, I would visit them as frequently as I could, often bringing along other writers and friends who were welcomed as special guests by the Reynolds.

My longest running and most intense contacts with them came after my own semi move to Mexico, where they had been living, as *emigratti* (becoming Mexican citizens legally), for some years. At the time it required eight years to become a Mexican citizen. They chose for their last residence, and one of the very few they had known for long periods of time, the quite sophisticated and elegant old world city of San Miguel de Allende, Guanajuato. An incredibly beautiful city, and a former silver-mining capitol of the world. It was delightfully Old World. . . you could have been walking down a street in Barcelona or Madrid for that matter. There were venerable old buildings of higher learning, libraries, theatres; everything needed to make for a perfect art colony.

The next-door city Guanajuato, Guanajuato is also filled with really unusual things like the mummies that so excited Ray Bradbury and an incredible underground cross-town freeway system running through what was the city sewer system 100 years earlier.

Nuñez 32 is a never-to-be-forgotten address. . . the street number of the Reynolds residence in Allende. It was Jeanette's masterwork. She was the complete Renaissance woman. I suspect there was nothing she couldn't do and accomplish at a master craftsman level or above.

Jeanette designed their house in detail. She acted as her own building superintendent and hired all the subcontractors by herself. She oversaw the construction of the house and made sure every detail was done to her exact specifications, and it was a beauty to behold. Once inside the entryway area and moving into the center courtyard patio, the first thing you saw were giant wooden doors some eight feet wide and ten feet tall. They are magnificent, hundreds of years old, made of hand-hewn wooden logs into different panels and framework, complete with ancient old iron hardware. It was the double entry doorway that had once graced the front of a very old and very isolated Catholic Church.

I once asked Mack where he got it but Mack just shrugged. "Some friends just dropped it off here once when they passed through town," he said.

I loved the courtyard area most about the house, filled as it was with large-leaf tropicals, fragrances of several flowers, gentle breezes, the twitterings of various birds, the trinkling of almost-silent running water, and the omnipresent tequila.

Mack and Jeanette Reynolds had a penchant for entertaining, holding always open houses for the "right" crowd, and that crowd consisted of every writer, agent, editor, artist, publisher, photographer, or model who could get close to them. It was always happy hour (and I have to admit that over time Mack really got to putting away the tequila from a bottomless imperial gallon bottle) inside their salon and it was always filled with big names that you recognize. . . people like Gary Jennings, Ted Cogswell, Dwight V. Swain, Avram Davidson, Martha and Henry Beck, Jerry Murray, Vivien Kern, and fragments of the Kemp entourages. Even the sleazebook writers loved Mack, taking to him as if he was their father.

It was a delightful drive from my house in Ajijic to Allende, a little less than 200 miles, and I made the trip as often as I could and as often as they would have me as a house guest. To get there was a pleasant trip across black-dirt-rich Irapuato, literally with "strawberry fields forever" reaching to the horizon in any direction. Along this route were numerous roadside vendors selling assorted baskets of fresh-picked strawberries or bottles of locally produced honey in assorted flavors. I would always pick up some selected berries and honey for Jeanette as I drove through the area. And, every time I would leave Allende going home, I would be loaded down with things like plants for my yard, delectable goodies to eat along the way, Thermos bottles filled with nectar. . . .

Needless to say, I loved them both dearly and miss them very much.

Earl Kemp
April 2009

RAMBLE HOUSE's

HARRY STEPHEN KEELER WEBWORK MYSTERIES

(RH) indicates the title is available ONLY in the **RAMBLE HOUSE** edition

The Ace of Spades Murder
The Affair of the Bottled Deuce (RH)
The Amazing Web
The Barking Clock
Behind That Mask
The Book with the Orange Leaves
The Bottle with the Green Wax Seal
The Box from Japan
The Case of the Canny Killer
The Case of the Crazy Corpse (RH)
The Case of the Flying Hands (RH)
The Case of the Ivory Arrow
The Case of the Jeweled Ragpicker
The Case of the Lavender Gripsack
The Case of the Mysterious Moll
The Case of the 16 Beans
The Case of the Transparent Nude (RH)
The Case of the Transposed Legs
The Case of the Two-Headed Idiot (RH)
The Case of the Two Strange Ladies
The Circus Stealers (RH)
Cleopatra's Tears
A Copy of Beowulf (RH)
The Crimson Cube (RH)
The Face of the Man From Saturn
Find the Clock
The Five Silver Buddhas
The 4th King
The Gallows Waits, My Lord! (RH)
The Green Jade Hand
Finger! Finger!
Hangman's Nights (RH)
I, Chameleon (RH)
I Killed Lincoln at 10:13! (RH)
The Iron Ring
The Man Who Changed His Skin (RH)
The Man with the Crimson Box
The Man with the Magic Eardrums
The Man with the Wooden Spectacles
The Marceau Case
The Matilda Hunter Murder
The Monocled Monster

The Murder of London Lew
The Murdered Mathematician
The Mysterious Card (RH)
The Mysterious Ivory Ball of Wong Shing
   Li (RH)
The Mystery of the Fiddling Cracksman
The Peacock Fan
The Photo of Lady X (RH)
The Portrait of Jirjohn Cobb
Report on Vanessa Hewstone (RH)
Riddle of the Travelling Skull
Riddle of the Wooden Parrakeet (RH)
The Scarlet Mummy (RH)
The Search for X-Y-Z
The Sharkskin Book
Sing Sing Nights
The Six From Nowhere (RH)
The Skull of the Waltzing Clown
The Spectacles of Mr. Cagliostro
Stand By—London Calling!
The Steeltown Strangler
The Stolen Gravestone (RH)
Strange Journey (RH)
The Strange Will
The Straw Hat Murders (RH)
The Street of 1000 Eyes (RH)
Thieves' Nights
Three Novellos (RH)
The Tiger Snake
The Trap (RH)
Vagabond Nights (Defrauded Yeggman)
Vagabond Nights 2 (10 Hours)
The Vanishing Gold Truck
The Voice of the Seven Sparrows
The Washington Square Enigma
When Thief Meets Thief
The White Circle (RH)
The Wonderful Scheme of Mr. Christopher
   Thorne
X. Jones—of Scotland Yard
Y. Cheung, Business Detective

Keeler Related Works

A To Izzard: A Harry Stephen Keeler Companion by Fender Tucker — Articles and stories about Harry, by Harry, and in his style. Included is a compleat bibliography.

Wild About Harry: Reviews of Keeler Novels — Edited by Richard Polt & Fender Tucker — 22 reviews of works by Harry Stephen Keeler from *Keeler News*. A perfect introduction to the author.

The Keeler Keyhole Collection: Annotated newsletter rants from Harry Stephen Keeler, edited by Francis M. Nevins. Over 400 pages of incredibly personal Keeleriana.

Fakealoo — Pastiches of the style of Harry Stephen Keeler by selected demented members of the HSK Society. Updated every year with the new winner.

RAMBLE HOUSE's OTHER LOONS

Strands of the Web: Short Stories of Harry Stephen Keeler — Edited and Introduced by Fred Cleaver

The Sam McCain Novels — Ed Gorman's terrific series includes *The Day the Music Died, Wake Up Little Susie* and *Will You Still Love Me Tomorrow?*

A Shot Rang Out — Three decades of reviews from Jon Breen

Blood Moon — The first of the Robert Payne series by Ed Gorman

The Time Armada — Fox B. Holden's 1953 SF gem.

Black River Falls — Suspense from the master, Ed Gorman

Sideslip — 1968 SF masterpiece by Ted White and Dave Van Arnam

The Triune Man — Mindscrambling science fiction from Richard A. Lupoff

Detective Duff Unravels It — Episodic mysteries by Harvey O'Higgins

Mysterious Martin, the Master of Murder — Two versions of a strange 1912 novel by Tod Robbins about a man who writes books that can kill.

The Master of Mysteries — 1912 novel of supernatural sleuthing by Gelett Burgess

Dago Red — 22 tales of dark suspense by Bill Pronzini

The Night Remembers — A 1991 Jack Walsh mystery from Ed Gorman

Rough Cut & New, Improved Murder — Ed Gorman's first two novels

Hollywood Dreams — A novel of the Depression by Richard O'Brien

Six Gelett Burgess Novels — *The Master of Mysteries, The White Cat, Two O'Clock Courage, Ladies in Boxes, Find the Woman, The Heart Line*

The Organ Reader — A huge compilation of just about everything published in the 1971-1972 radical bay-area newspaper, *THE ORGAN*.

A Clear Path to Cross — Sharon Knowles short mystery stories by Ed Lynskey

Old Times' Sake — Short stories by James Reasoner from Mike Shayne Magazine

Freaks and Fantasies — Eerie tales by Tod Robbins, collaborator of Tod Browning on the film FREAKS.

Five Jim Harmon Sleaze Double Novels — *Vixen Hollow/Celluloid Scandal, The Man Who Made Maniacs/Silent Siren, Ape Rape/Wanton Witch, Sex Burns Like Fire/Twist Session*, and *Sudden Lust/Passion Strip*. More doubles to come!

Marblehead: A Novel of H.P. Lovecraft — A long-lost masterpiece from Richard A. Lupoff. Published for the first time!

The Compleat Ova Hamlet — Parodies of SF authors by Richard A. Lupoff New edition!

The Secret Adventures of Sherlock Holmes — Three Sherlockian pastiches by the Brooklyn author/publisher, Gary Lovisi.

The Universal Holmes — Richard A. Lupoff's 2007 collection of five Holmesian pastiches and a recipe for giant rat stew.

Four Joel Townsley Rogers Novels — By the author of *The Red Right Hand: Once In a Red Moon, Lady With the Dice, The Stopped Clock, Never Leave My Bed*

Two Joel Townsley Rogers Story Collections — Night of Horror and Killing Time

Twenty Norman Berrow Novels — *The Bishop's Sword, Ghost House, Don't Go Out After Dark, Claws of the Cougar, The Smokers of Hashish, The Secret Dancer, Don't Jump Mr. Boland!, The Footprints of Satan, Fingers for Ransom, The Three Tiers of Fantasy, The Spaniard's Thumb, The Eleventh Plague, Words Have Wings, One Thrilling Night, The Lady's in Danger, It Howls at Night, The Terror in the Fog, Oil Under the Window, Murder in the Melody, The Singing Room*

The N. R. De Mexico Novels — Robert Bragg presents *Marijuana Girl, Madman on a Drum, Private Chauffeur* in one volume.

Four Chelsea Quinn Yarbro Novels featuring Charlie Moon — *Ogilvie, Tallant and Moon, Music When the Sweet Voice Dies, Poisonous Fruit* and *Dead Mice*

Four Walter S. Masterman Mysteries — *The Green Toad, The Flying Beast, The Yellow Mistletoe* and *The Wrong Verdict*, fantastic impossible plots. More to come.

Two Hake Talbot Novels — *Rim of the Pit, The Hangman's Handyman*. Classic locked room mysteries.

Two Alexander Laing Novels — *The Motives of Nicholas Holtz* and *Dr. Scarlett*, stories of medical mayhem and intrigue from the 30s.

Four David Hume Novels — *Corpses Never Argue, Cemetery First Stop, Make Way for the Mourners, Eternity Here I Come*, and more to come.

Three Wade Wright Novels — *Echo of Fear, Death At Nostalgia Street* and *It Leads to Murder*, with more to come!

Six Rupert Penny Novels — *Policeman's Holiday, Policeman's Evidence, Lucky Policeman, Policeman in Armour, Sealed Room Murder, Sweet Poison*, classic mysteries.

Five Jack Mann Novels — Strange murder in the English countryside. *Gees' First Case, Nightmare Farm, Grey Shapes, The Ninth Life, The Glass Too Many.*

Seven Max Afford Novels — *Owl of Darkness, Death's Mannikins, Blood on His Hands, The Dead Are Blind, The Sheep and the Wolves, Sinners in Paradise* and *Two Locked Room Mysteries and a Ripping Yarn* by one of Australia's finest novelists.

Five Joseph Shallit Novels — *The Case of the Billion Dollar Body, Lady Don't Die on My Doorstep, Kiss the Killer, Yell Bloody Murder, Take Your Last Look.* One of America's best 50's authors.

Two Crimson Clown Novels — By Johnston McCulley, author of the Zorro novels, *The Crimson Clown* and *The Crimson Clown Again.*

The Best of 10-Story Book — edited by Chris Mikul, over 35 stories from the literary magazine Harry Stephen Keeler edited.

A Young Man's Heart — A forgotten early classic by Cornell Woolrich

The Anthony Boucher Chronicles — edited by Francis M. Nevins
   Book reviews by Anthony Boucher written for the *San Francisco Chronicle,* 1942 – 1947. Essential and fascinating reading.

Muddled Mind: Complete Works of Ed Wood, Jr. — David Hayes and Hayden Davis deconstruct the life and works of a mad genius.

Gadsby — A lipogram (a novel without the letter E). Ernest Vincent Wright's last work, published in 1939 right before his death.

My First Time: The One Experience You Never Forget — Michael Birchwood — 64 true first-person narratives of how they lost it.

Automaton — Brilliant treatise on robotics: 1928-style! By H. Stafford Hatfield

The Incredible Adventures of Rowland Hern — Rousing 1928 impossible crimes by Nicholas Olde.

Slammer Days — Two full-length prison memoirs: *Men into Beasts* (1952) by George Sylvester Viereck and *Home Away From Home* (1962) by Jack Woodford

Murder in Black and White — 1931 classic tennis whodunit by Evelyn Elder

Killer's Caress — Cary Moran's 1936 hardboiled thriller

The Golden Dagger — 1951 Scotland Yard yarn by E. R. Punshon

Beat Books #1 — Two beatnik classics, *A Sea of Thighs* by Ray Kainen and *Village Hipster* by J.X. Williams

A Smell of Smoke — 1951 English countryside thriller by Miles Burton

Ruled By Radio — 1925 futuristic novel by Robert L. Hadfield & Frank E. Farncombe

Murder in Silk — A 1937 Yellow Peril novel of the silk trade by Ralph Trevor

The Case of the Withered Hand — 1936 potboiler by John G. Brandon

Finger-prints Never Lie — A 1939 classic detective novel by John G. Brandon

Inclination to Murder — 1966 thriller by New Zealand's Harriet Hunter

Invaders from the Dark — Classic werewolf tale from Greye La Spina

Fatal Accident — Murder by automobile, a 1936 mystery by Cecil M. Wills

The Devil Drives — A prison and lost treasure novel by Virgil Markham

Dr. Odin — Douglas Newton's 1933 potboiler comes back to life.

The Chinese Jar Mystery — Murder in the manor by John Stephen Strange, 1934

The Julius Caesar Murder Case — A classic 1935 re-telling of the assassination by Wallace Irwin that's much more fun than the Shakespeare version

West Texas War and Other Western Stories — by Gary Lovisi

The Contested Earth and Other SF Stories — A never-before published space opera and seven short stories by Jim Harmon.

Tales of the Macabre and Ordinary — Modern twisted horror by Chris Mikul, author of the *Bizarrism* series.

The Gold Star Line — Seaboard adventure from L.T. Reade and Robert Eustace.

The Werewolf vs the Vampire Woman — Hard to believe ultraviolence by either Arthur M. Scarm or Arthur M. Scram.

Black Hogan Strikes Again — Australia's Peter Renwick pens a tale of the outback.

Don Diablo: Book of a Lost Film — Two-volume treatment of a western by Paul Landres, with diagrams. Intro by Francis M. Nevins.

The Charlie Chaplin Murder Mystery — Movie hijinks by Wes D. Gehring

The Koky Comics — A collection of all of the 1978-1981 Sunday and daily comic strips by Richard O'Brien and Mort Gerberg, in two volumes.

Suzy — Another collection of comic strips from Richard O'Brien and Bob Vojtko

Dime Novels: Ramble House's 10-Cent Books — *Knife in the Dark* by Robert Leslie Bellem, *Hot Lead* and *Song of Death* by Ed Earl Repp, *A Hashish House in New York* by H.H. Kane, and five more.

Blood in a Snap — The *Finnegan's Wake* of the 21ˢᵗ century, by Jim Weiler and Al Gorithm

Stakeout on Millennium Drive — Award-winning Indianapolis Noir — Ian Woollen.

Dope Tales #1 — Two dope-riddled classics; *Dope Runners* by Gerald Grantham and *Death Takes the Joystick* by Phillip Condé.

Dope Tales #2 — Two more narco-classics; *The Invisible Hand* by Rex Dark and *The Smokers of Hashish* by Norman Berrow.

Dope Tales #3 — Two enchanting novels of opium by the master, Sax Rohmer. *Dope* and *The Yellow Claw.*

Tenebrae — Ernest G. Henham's 1898 horror tale brought back.

The Singular Problem of the Stygian House-Boat — Two classic tales by John Kendrick Bangs about the denizens of Hades.

Tiresias — Psychotic modern horror novel by Jonathan M. Sweet.

The One After Snelling — Kickass modern noir from Richard O'Brien.

The Sign of the Scorpion — 1935 Edmund Snell tale of oriental evil.

The House of the Vampire — 1907 poetic thriller by George S. Viereck.

An Angel in the Street — Modern hardboiled noir by Peter Genovese.

The Devil's Mistress — Scottish gothic tale by J. W. Brodie-Innes.

The Lord of Terror — 1925 mystery with master-criminal, Fantômas.

The Lady of the Terraces — 1925 adventure by E. Charles Vivian.

My Deadly Angel — 1955 Cold War drama by John Chelton.

Prose Bowl — Futuristic satire — Bill Pronzini & Barry N. Malzberg .

Satan's Den Exposed — True crime in Truth or Consequences New Mexico — Award-winning journalism by the *Desert Journal.*

The Amorous Intrigues & Adventures of Aaron Burr — by Anonymous — Hot historical action.

I Stole $16,000,000 — A true story by cracksman Herbert E. Wilson.

The Black Dark Murders — Vintage 50s college murder yarn by Milt Ozaki, writing as Robert O. Saber.

Sex Slave — Potboiler of lust in the days of Cleopatra — Dion Leclerq.

You'll Die Laughing — Bruce Elliott's 1945 novel of murder at a practical joker's English countryside manor.

The Private Journal & Diary of John H. Surratt — The memoirs of the man who conspired to assassinate President Lincoln.

Dead Man Talks Too Much — Hollywood boozer by Weed Dickenson.

Red Light — History of legal prostitution in Shreveport Louisiana by Eric Brock. Includes wonderful photos of the houses and the ladies.

A Snark Selection — Lewis Carroll's *The Hunting of the Snark* with two Snarkian chapters by Harry Stephen Keeler — Illustrated by Gavin L. O'Keefe.

Ripped from the Headlines! — The Jack the Ripper story as told in the newspaper articles in the *New York* and *London Times.*

Geronimo — S. M. Barrett's 1905 autobiography of a noble American.

The White Peril in the Far East — Sidney Lewis Gulick's 1905 indictment of the West and assurance that Japan would never attack the U.S.

The Compleat Calhoon — All of Fender Tucker's works: Includes *The Totah Trilogy, Weed, Women and Song* and *Tales from the Tower,* plus a CD of all of his songs.

RAMBLE HOUSE

Fender Tucker, Prop.

www.ramblehouse.com   fender@ramblehouse.com

228-826-1783   10329 Sheephead Drive, Vancleave MS 39565